CARL SANDBURG

Rootabaga Stories

Part One

ILLUSTRATIONS AND DECORATIONS BY
MAUD AND MISKA PETERSHAM

A Voyager Book

Harcourt Brace Jovanovich, Inc., New York

TO SPINK AND SKABOOTCH

Printed in the United States of America

A B C D E F G H I J

Library of Congress Cataloging in Publication Data

Sandburg, Carl, 1878-1967.
Rootabaga stories.

(A Voyager book, AVB 85, AVB 90)
SUMMARY: A two-volume collection of fanciful,
humorous short stories introducing such characters as
the Potato Face Blind Man, Henry Hagglyhoagly, the
Blue Wind Boy, Googler and Gaggler, and others.
CONTENTS: pt. 1. Rootabaga stories.—pt. 2.
Rootabaga pigeons.
1. Children's stories. [1. Short stories.
2. Fantasy] I. Petersham, Maud (Fuller) 1890-1971,
illus. II. Petersham, Miska, 1888-1960, illus.
III. Title.
PZ7.S1965Ro12   813'.5'2   [Fic]   73-13875
ISBN 0-15-678900-0 (v. 1)

CONTENTS

Contents

4.

Four Stories About the Deep Doom of Dark Doorways

5.

Three Stories About Three Ways the Wind Went Winding

6.

Four Stories About Dear, Dear Eyes

Contents

7.

One Story—"Only the Fire-Born Understand Blue"

8.

Two Stories About Corn Fairies, Blue Foxes, Flongboos and Happenings That Happened in the
United States and Canada

v

FULL-PAGE ILLUSTRATIONS

1. Three Stories About the Finding of the Zigzag Railroad, the Pigs with Bibs On, the Circus Clown Ovens, the Village of Liver-and-Onions, the Village of Cream Puffs.

People: Gimme the Ax

Please Gimme

Ax Me No Questions

The Ticket Agent

Wing Tip the Spick

The Four Uncles

The Rat in a Blizzard

The Five Rusty Rats

More People:

Balloon Pickers

Baked Clowns

Polka Dot Pigs

How They Broke Away to Go to the Rootabaga Country

Gimme the Ax lived in a house where everything is the same as it always was.

"The chimney sits on top of the house and lets the smoke out," said Gimme the Ax. "The doorknobs open the doors. The windows are always either open or shut. We are always either upstairs or downstairs in this house. Everything is the same as it always was."

So he decided to let his children name themselves.

"The first words they speak as soon as they learn to make words shall be their names," he said. "They shall name themselves."

When the first boy came to the house of Gimme the Ax, he was named Please Gimme. When the first girl came she was named Ax Me No Questions.

And both of the children had the shadows of valleys by night in their eyes and the lights of early morning, when the sun is coming up, on their foreheads.

And the hair on top of their heads was a dark wild grass. And they loved to turn the doorknobs, open the doors, and run out to have the wind comb their hair and touch their eyes and put its six soft fingers on their foreheads.

And then because no more boys came and no more girls came, Gimme the Ax said to himself, "My first boy is my last and my last girl is my first and they picked their names themselves."

To the Rootabaga Country

Please Gimme grew up and his ears got longer. Ax Me No Questions grew up and her ears got longer. And they kept on living in the house where everything is the same as it always was. They learned to say just as their father said, "The chimney sits on top of the house and lets the smoke out, the doorknobs open the doors, the windows are always either open or shut, we are always either upstairs or downstairs—everything is the same as it always was."

After a while they began asking each other in the cool of the evening after they had eggs for breakfast in the morning, "Who's who? How much? And what's the answer?"

"It is too much to be too long anywhere," said the tough old man, Gimme the Ax.

And Please Gimme and Ax Me No Questions, the tough son and the tough daughter of Gimme the Ax, answered their father, "It *is* too much to be too long anywhere."

So they sold everything they had, pigs, pastures, pepper pickers, pitchforks, everything except their ragbags and a few extras.

When their neighbors saw them selling everything they had, the different neighbors said, "They are going to Kansas, to Kokomo, to Canada, to Kankakee, to Kalamazoo, to Kamchatka, to the Chattahoochee."

One little sniffer with his eyes half shut and a mitten on his nose, laughed in his hat five ways and said, "They are going to the moon and when they get there they will find everything is the same as it always was."

All the spot cash money he got for selling everything, pigs, pastures, pepper pickers, pitchforks, Gimme the Ax put in a ragbag and slung on his back like a rag picker going home.

Then he took Please Gimme, his oldest and youngest and only son, and Ax Me No Questions, his oldest and youngest and only daughter, and went to the railroad station.

The ticket agent was sitting at the window selling railroad tickets the same as always.

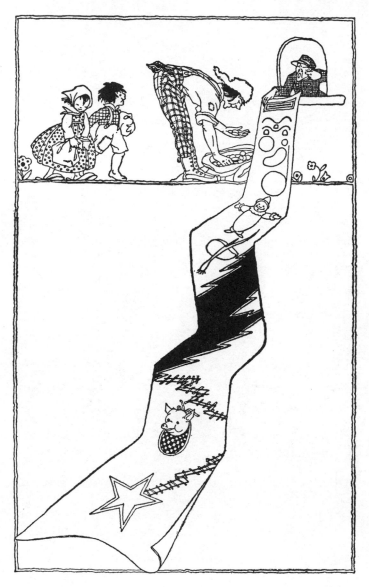

He opened the ragbag and took out all the
spot cash money

"Do you wish a ticket to go away and come back or do you wish a ticket to go away and *never* come back?" the ticket agent asked wiping sleep out of his eyes.

"We wish a ticket to ride where the railroad tracks run off into the sky and never come back—send us far as the railroad rails go and then forty ways farther yet," was the reply of Gimme the Ax.

"So far? So early? So soon?" asked the ticket agent wiping more sleep out his eyes. "Then I will give you a new ticket. It blew in. It is a long slick yellow leather slab ticket with a blue spanch across it."

Gimme the Ax thanked the ticket agent once, thanked the ticket agent twice, and then instead of thanking the ticket agent three times he opened the ragbag and took out all the spot cash money he got for selling everything, pigs, pastures, pepper pickers, pitchforks, and paid the spot cash money to the ticket agent.

Before he put it in his pocket he looked once,

twice, three times at the long yellow leather slab ticket with a blue spanch across it.

Then with Please Gimme and Ax Me No Questions he got on the railroad train, showed the conductor his ticket and they started to ride to where the railroad tracks run off into the blue sky and then forty ways farther yet.

The train ran on and on. It came to the place where the railroad tracks run off into the blue sky. And it ran on and on chick chick-a-chick chick-a-chick chick-a-chick.

Sometimes the engineer hooted and tooted the whistle. Sometimes the fireman rang the bell. Sometimes the open-and-shut of the steam hog's nose choked and spit pfisty-pfoost, pfisty-pfoost, pfisty-pfoost. But no matter what happened to the whistle and the bell and the steam hog, the train ran on and on to where the railroad tracks run off into the blue sky. And then it ran on and on more and more.

Sometimes Gimme the Ax looked in his pocket, put his fingers in and took out the long slick yellow leather slab ticket with a blue spanch across it.

"Not even the Kings of Egypt with all their climbing camels, and all their speedy, spotted, lucky lizards, ever had a ride like this," he said to his children.

Then something happened. They met another train running on the same track. One train was going one way. The other was going the other way. They met. They passed each other.

"What was it—what happened?" the children asked their father.

"One train went over, the other train went under," he answered. "This is the Over and Under country. Nobody gets out of the way of anybody else. They either go over or under."

Next they came to the country of the balloon pickers. Hanging down from the sky strung on strings so fine the eye could not see them at first, was the balloon crop of that summer. The sky was thick with balloons. Red, blue, yellow balloons, white, purple and orange balloons—peach, watermelon and potato bal- loons—rye loaf and wheat loaf balloons—link sausage and pork chop balloons—they floated and filled the sky.

The balloon pickers were walking on high stilts picking balloons. Each picker had his own stilts, long or short. For picking balloons near the ground he had short stilts. If he wanted to pick far and high he walked on a far and high pair of stilts.

Baby pickers on baby stilts were picking baby balloons. When they fell off the stilts the handful of balloons they were holding kept them in the air till they got their feet into the stilts again.

"Who is that away up there in the sky climb- ing like a bird in the morning?" Ax Me No Questions asked her father.

"He was singing too happy," replied the father. "The songs came out of his neck and made him so light the balloons pulled him off his stilts."

"Will he ever come down again back to his own people?"

"Yes, his heart will get heavy when his songs are all gone. Then he will drop down to his stilts again."

The train was running on and on. The engineer hooted and tooted the whistle when he felt like it. The fireman rang the bell when he felt that way. And sometimes the open-and-shut of the steam hog had to go pfisty-pfoost, pfisty-pfoost.

"Next is the country where the circus clowns come from," said Gimme the Ax to his son and daughter. "Keep your eyes open."

They did keep their eyes open. They saw cities with ovens, long and short ovens, fat stubby ovens, lean lank ovens, all for baking either long or short clowns, or fat and stubby or lean and lank clowns.

After each clown was baked in the oven it

was taken out into the sunshine and put up to stand like a big white doll with a red mouth leaning against the fence.

Two men came along to each baked clown standing still like a doll. One man threw a bucket of white fire over it. The second man pumped a wind pump with a living red wind through the red mouth.

The clown rubbed his eyes, opened his mouth, twisted his neck, wiggled his ears, wriggled his toes, jumped away from the fence and began turning handsprings, cartwheels, somersaults and flipflops in the sawdust ring near the fence.

"The next we come to is the Rootabaga Country where the big city is the Village of Liver-and-Onions," said Gimme the Ax, looking again in his pocket to be sure he had the long slick yellow leather slab ticket with a blue spanch across it.

The train ran on and on till it stopped running straight and began running in zigzags like one letter Z put next to another Z and the next and the next.

The tracks and the rails and the ties and the spikes under the train all stopped being straight and changed to zigzags like one letter Z and another letter Z put next after the other.

"It seems like we go half way and then back up," said Ax Me No Questions.

"Look out of the window and see if the pigs have bibs on," said Gimme the Ax. "If the pigs are wearing bibs then this is the Rootabaga country."

And they looked out of the zigzagging windows of the zigzagging cars and the first pigs they saw had bibs on. And the next pigs and the next pigs they saw all had bibs on.

The checker pigs had checker bibs on, the striped pigs had striped bibs on. And the polka dot pigs had polka dot bibs on.

"Who fixes it for the pigs to have bibs on?" Please Gimme asked his father.

"The fathers and mothers fix it," answered

Gimme the Ax. "The checker pigs have checker fathers and mothers. The striped pigs have striped fathers and mothers. And the polka dot pigs have polka dot fathers and mothers."

And the train went zigzagging on and on running on the tracks and the rails and the spikes and the ties which were all zigzag like the letter Z and the letter Z.

And after a while the train zigzagged on into the Village of Liver-and-Onions, known as the biggest city in the big, big Rootabaga country.

And so if you are going to the Rootabaga country you will know when you get there because the railroad tracks change from straight to zigzag, the pigs have bibs on and it is the fathers and mothers who fix it.

And if you start to go to that country remember first you must sell everything you have, pigs, pastures, pepper pickers, pitchforks, put the spot cash money in a ragbag and go to the railroad station and ask the ticket agent for a long slick yellow leather slab ticket with a blue spanch across it.

And you mustn't be surprised if the ticket agent wipes sleep from his eyes and asks, "So far? So early? So soon?"

How They Bring Back the Village of Cream Puffs When the Wind Blows It Away

A girl named Wing Tip the Spick came to the Village of Liver-and-Onions to visit her uncle and her uncle's uncle on her mother's side and her uncle and her uncle's uncle on her father's side.

It was the first time the four uncles had a chance to see their little relation, their niece. Each one of the four uncles was proud of the blue eyes of Wing Tip the Spick.

How They Bring Back Village

The two uncles on her mother's side took a long deep look into her blue eyes and said, "Her eyes are so blue, such a clear light blue, they are the same as cornflowers with blue raindrops shining and dancing on silver leaves after a sun shower in any of the summer months."

And the two uncles on her father's side, after taking a long deep look into the eyes of Wing Tip the Spick, said, "Her eyes are so blue, such a clear light shining blue, they are the same as cornflowers with blue raindrops shining and dancing on the silver leaves after a sun shower in any of the summer months."

And though Wing Tip the Spick didn't listen and didn't hear what the uncles said about her blue eyes, she did say to herself when they were not listening, "I know these are sweet uncles and I am going to have a sweet time visiting my relations."

The four uncles said to her, "Will you let us ask you two questions, first the first question and second the second question?"

Then the uncles asked her the first question **first**

"I will let you ask me fifty questions this morning, fifty questions tomorrow morning, and fifty questions any morning. I like to listen to questions. They slip in one ear and slip out of the other."

Then the uncles asked her the first question first, "Where do you come from?" and the second question second, "Why do you have two freckles on your chin?"

"Answering your first question first," said Wing Tip the Spick, "I come from the Village of Cream Puffs, a little light village on the upland corn prairie. From a long ways off it looks like a little hat you could wear on the end of your thumb to keep the rain off your thumb."

"Tell us more," said one uncle. "Tell us much," said another uncle. "Tell it without stopping," added another uncle. "Interruptions nix nix," murmured the last of the uncles.

"It is a light little village on the upland corn prairie many miles past the sunset in the west,"

23

went on Wing Tip the Spick. "It is light the same as a cream puff is light. It sits all by itself on the big long prairie where the prairie goes up in a slope. There on the slope the winds play around the village. They sing it wind songs, summer wind songs in summer, winter wind songs in winter."

"And sometimes like an accident, the wind gets rough. And when the wind gets rough it picks up the little Village of Cream Puffs and blows it away off in the sky—all by itself."

"O-o-h-h," said one uncle. "Um-m-m-m," said the other three uncles.

"Now the people in the village all understand the winds with their wind songs in summer and winter. And they understand the rough wind who comes sometimes and picks up the village and blows it away off high in the sky all by itself.

"If you go to the public square in the middle of the village you will see a big roundhouse. If you take the top off the roundhouse you will see a big spool with a long string winding up around the spool.

"Now whenever the rough wind comes and picks up the village and blows it away off high in the sky all by itself then the string winds loose off the spool, because the village is fastened to the string. So the rough wind blows and blows and the string on the spool winds looser and looser the farther the village goes blowing away off into the sky all by itself.

"Then at last when the rough wind, so forgetful, so careless, has had all the fun it wants, then the people of the village all come together and begin to wind up the spool and bring back the village where it was before."

"O-o-h-h," said one uncle. "Um-m-m-m," said the other three uncles.

"And sometimes when you come to the village to see your little relation, your niece who has four such sweet uncles, maybe she will lead you through the middle of the city to the public square and show you the roundhouse. They call it the Roundhouse of the Big Spool. And they are proud because it was thought up and is there to show when visitors come."

"And now will you answer the second question second—why do you have two freckles on your chin?" interrupted the uncle who had said before, "Interruptions nix nix."

"The freckles are put on," answered Wing Tip the Spick. "When a girl goes away from the Village of Cream Puffs her mother puts on two freckles, on the chin. Each freckle must be the same as a little burnt cream puff kept in the oven too long. After the two freckles looking like two little burnt cream puffs are put on her chin, they remind the girl every morning when she combs her hair and looks in the looking glass. They remind her where she came from and she mustn't stay away too long."

"O-h-h-h," said one uncle. "Um-m-m-m," said the other three uncles. And they talked among each other afterward, the four uncles by themselves, saying:

26

"She has a gift. It is her eyes. They are so blue, such a clear light blue, the same as cornflowers with blue raindrops shining and dancing on silver leaves after a sun shower in any of the summer months."

At the same time Wing Tip the Spick was saying to herself, "I know for sure now these are sweet uncles and I am going to have a sweet time visiting my relations."

How the Five Rusty Rats Helped Find a New Village

One day while Wing Tip the Spick was visiting her four uncles in the Village of Liver-and-Onions, a blizzard came up. Snow filled the sky and the wind blew and made a noise like heavy wagon axles grinding and crying.

And on this day a gray rat came to the house of the four uncles, a rat with gray skin and gray hair, gray as the gray gravy on a beefsteak. The rat had a basket. In the basket was a catfish. And the rat said, "Please let me have a ·little fire and a little salt as I wish to make a little bowl of hot catfish soup to keep me warm through the blizzard."

And the four uncles all said together, "This is no time for rats to be around—and we would like to ask you where you got the catfish in the basket."

"Oh, oh, oh, please—in the name of the five rusty rats, the five lucky rats of the Village of Cream Puffs, please don't," was the exclamation of Wing Tip the Spick.

The uncles stopped. They looked long and deep into the eyes of Wing Tip the Spick and thought, as they had thought before, how her eyes were clear light blue the same as cornflowers with blue raindrops shining on the silver leaves in a summer sun shower.

And the four uncles opened the door and let the gray rat come in with the basket and the catfish. They showed the gray rat the way to the kitchen and the fire and the salt. And they watched the rat and kept him company while he fixed himself a catfish soup to keep him warm traveling through the blizzard with the sky full of snow.

After they opened the front door and let the rat out and said good-by, they turned to Wing Tip the Spick and asked her to tell them about the five rusty lucky rats of the Village of Cream Puffs where she lived with her father and her mother and her folks.

"When I was a little girl growing up, before I learned all I learned since I got older, my grandfather gave me a birthday present because I was nine years old. I remember how he said to me, 'You will never be nine years old again after this birthday, so I give you this box for a birthday present.'

"In the box was a pair of red slippers with a gold clock on each slipper. One of the clocks ran fast. The other clock ran slow. And he told me if I wished to be early anywhere I should go by the clock that ran fast. And if I wished to be late anywhere I should go by the clock that ran slow.

31

"And that same birthday he took me down through the middle of the Village of Cream Puffs to the public square near the Roundhouse of the Big Spool. There he pointed his finger at the statue of the five rusty rats, the five lucky rats. And as near as I can remember his words, he said:

" 'Many years ago, long before the snow birds began to wear funny little slip-on hats and funny little slip-on shoes, and away back long before the snow birds learned how to slip off their slip-on hats and how to slip off their slip-on shoes, long ago in the faraway Village of Liver-and-Onions, the people who ate cream puffs came together and met in the streets and picked up their baggage and put their belongings on their shoulders and marched out of the Village of Liver-and-Onions saying, "We shall find a new place for a village and the name of it shall be the Village of Cream Puffs.

" 'They marched out on the prairie with their baggage and belongings in sacks on their

32

They held on to the long curved tails of
the rusty rats

shoulders. And a blizzard came up. Snow filled the sky. The wind blew and blew and made a noise like heavy wagon axles grinding and crying.

" 'The snow came on. The wind twisted all day and all night and all the next day. The wind changed black and twisted and spit icicles in their faces. They got lost in the blizzard. They expected to die and be buried in the snow for the wolves to come and eat them.

" 'Then the five lucky rats came, the five rusty rats, rust on their skin and hair, rust on their feet and noses, rust all over, and especially, most especially of all, rust on their long curved tails. They dug their noses down into the snow and their long curved tails stuck up far above the snow where the people who were lost in the blizzard could take hold of the tails like handles.

" 'And so, while the wind and the snow blew and the blizzard beat its icicles in their faces, they held on to the long curved tails of the rusty rats till they came to the place where the Village of Cream Puffs now stands. It was the rusty rats who saved their lives and showed them where to put their new village. That is why this statue now stands in the public square, this statue of the shapes of the five rusty rats, the five lucky rats with their noses down in the snow and their long curved tails lifted high out of the snow.'

"That is the story as my grandfather told it to me. And he said it happened long ago, long before the snow birds began to wear slip-on hats and slip-on shoes, long before they learned how to slip off the slip-on hats and to slip off the slip-on shoes."

"O-h-h-h," said one of the uncles. "Um-m-m-m," said the other three uncles.

"And sometime," added Wing Tip the Spick, "when you go away from the Village of Liver-and-Onions and cross the Shampoo River and ride many miles across the upland prairie till you come to the Village of Cream Puffs, you will find a girl there who loves four uncles very much.

"And if you ask her politely, she will show you the red slippers with gold clocks on them, one clock to be early by, the other to be late by. And if you are still more polite she will take you through the middle of the town to the public square and show you the statue of the five rusty lucky rats with their long curved tails sticking up in the air like handles. And the tails are curved so long and so nice you will feel like going up and taking hold of them to see what will happen to you."

2. Five Stories About the Potato Face Blind Man

People: The Potato Face Blind Man
Any Ice Today
Pick Ups
Lizzie Lazarus
Poker Face the Baboon
Hot Dog the Tiger
Whitson Whimble
A Man Shoveling Money
A Watermelon Moon
White Gold Boys
Blue Silver Girls
Big White Moon Spiders
Zizzies
Gimme the Ax Again

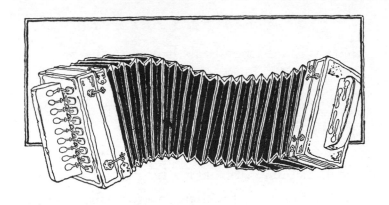

The Potato Face Blind Man Who Lost the Diamond Rabbit on His Gold Accordion

There was a Potato Face Blind Man used to play an accordion on the Main Street corner nearest the postoffice in the Village of Liver-and-Onions.

Any Ice Today came along and said, "It looks like it used to be an 18 carat gold accordion with rich pawnshop diamonds in it; it looks like it used to be a grand accordion once and not so grand now."

"Oh, yes, oh, yes, it was gold all over on the outside," said the Potato Face Blind Man, "and there was a diamond rabbit next to the handles on each side, two diamond rabbits."

"How do you mean diamond rabbits?" Any Ice Today asked.

"Ears, legs, head, feet, ribs, tail, all fixed out in diamonds to make a nice rabbit with his diamond chin on his diamond toenails. When I play good pieces so people cry hearing my accordion music, then I put my fingers over and feel of the rabbit's diamond chin on his diamond toenails, 'Attaboy, li'l bunny, attaboy, li'l bunny.'"

"Yes I hear you talking but it is like dream talking. I wonder why your accordion looks like somebody stole it and took it to a pawnshop and took it out and somebody stole it again and took it to a pawnshop and took it out and somebody stole it again. And they kept on stealing it and taking it out of the pawnshop and stealing it again till the gold wore off so it looks like a used-to-be-yesterday."

"Oh, yes, o-h, y-e-s, you are right. It is not

like the accordion it used to be. It knows more knowledge than it used to know just the same as this Potato Face Blind Man knows more knowledge than he used to know."

"Tell me about it," said Any Ice Today.

"It is simple. If a blind man plays an accordion on the street to make people cry it makes them sad and when they are sad the gold goes away off the accordion. And if a blind man goes to sleep because his music is full of sleepy songs like the long wind in a sleepy valley, then while the blind man is sleeping the diamonds in the diamond rabbit all go away. I play a sleepy song and go to sleep and I wake up and the diamond ear of the diamond rabbit is gone. I play another sleepy song and go to sleep and wake up and the diamond tail of the diamond rabbit is gone. After a while all the diamond rabbits are gone, even the diamond chin sitting on the diamond toenails of the rabbits next to the handles of the accordion, even those are gone."

The Potato Face Blind Man

"Is there anything I can do?" asked Any Ice Today.

"I do it myself," said the Potato Face Blind Man. "If I am too sorry I just play the sleepy song of the long wind going up the sleepy valleys. And that carries me away where I have time and money to dream about the new wonderful accordions and postoffices where everybody that gets a letter and everybody that don't get a letter stops and remembers the Potato Face Blind Man."

How the Potato Face Blind Man Enjoyed Himself on a Fine Spring Morning

On a Friday morning when the flummywisters were yodeling yisters high in the elm trees, the Potato Face Blind Man came down to his work sitting at the corner nearest the postoffice in the Village of Liver-and-Onions and playing his gold-that-used-to-be accordion for the pleasure of the ears of the people going into the postoffice to see if they got any letters for themselves or their families.

"It is a good day, a lucky day," said the Potato Face Blind Man, "because for a beginning I have heard high in the elm trees the flummywisters yodeling their yisters in the long branches of the lingering leaves. So—so— I am going to listen to myself playing on my accordion the same yisters, the same yodels, drawing them like long glad breathings out of my glad accordion, long breathings of the branches of the lingering leaves."

And he sat down in his chair. On the sleeve of his coat he tied a sign, "I Am Blind *Too*." On the top button of his coat he hung a little thimble. On the bottom button of his coat he hung a tin copper cup. On the middle button he hung a wooden mug. By the side of him on the left side on the sidewalk he put a galvanized iron washtub, and on the right side an aluminum dishpan.

"It is a good day, a lucky day, and I am sure many people will stop and remember the Potato Face Blind Man," he sang to himself like a little song as he began running his fingers up and down the keys of the accordion like the

46

"I am sure many people will stop and remember the
Potato Face Blind Man"

yisters of the lingering leaves in the elm trees.

Then came Pick Ups. Always it happened Pick Ups asked questions and wished to know. And so this is how the questions and answers ran when the Potato Face filled the ears of Pick Ups with explanations.

"What is the piece you are playing on the keys of your accordion so fast sometimes, so slow sometimes, so sad some of the moments, so glad some of the moments?"

"It is the song the mama flummywisters sing when they button loose the winter underwear of the baby flummywisters and sing:

"Fly, you little flummies,
Sing, you little wisters."

"And why do you have a little thimble on the top button of your coat?"

"That is for the dimes to be put in. Some people see it and say, 'Oh, I must put in a whole thimbleful of dimes.'"

"And the tin copper cup?"

"That is for the base ball players to stand off ten feet and throw in nickels and pennies. The one who throws the most into the cup will be the most lucky."

"And the wooden mug?"

"There is a hole in the bottom of it. The hole is as big as the bottom. The nickel goes in and comes out again. It is for the very poor people who wish to give me a nickel and yet get the nickel back."

"The aluminum dishpan and the galvanized iron washtub—what are they doing by the side of you on both sides on the sidewalk?"

"Sometime maybe it will happen everybody who goes into the postoffice and comes out will stop and pour out all their money, because they might get afraid their money is no good any more. If such a happening ever happens then it will be nice for the people to have some place to pour their money. Such is the explanation why you see the aluminum dishpan and galvanized iron tub."

"Explain your sign—why is it, 'I Am Blind *Too*.'"

"Oh, I am sorry to explain to you, Pick Ups, why this is so which. Some of the people who pass by here going into the postoffice and coming out, they have eyes—but they see nothing with their eyes. They look where they are going and they get where they wish to get, but they forget why they came and they do not know how to come away. They are my blind brothers. It is for them I have the sign that reads, 'I Am Blind *Too*.'"

"I have my ears full of explanations and I thank you," said Pick Ups.

"Good-by," said the Potato Face Blind Man as he began drawing long breathings like lingering leaves out of the accordion—along with the song the mama flummywisters sing when they button loose the winter underwear of the baby flummywisters.

Poker Face the Baboon and Hot Dog
the Tiger

When the moon has a green rim with red
meat inside and black seeds on the red meat,
then in the Rootabaga Country they call it a
Watermelon Moon and look for anything to
happen.

It was a night when a Watermelon Moon was
shining. Lizzie Lazarus came to the upstairs
room of the Potato Face Blind Man. Poker
Face the Baboon and Hot Dog the Tiger were
with her. She was leading them with a pink
string.

"You see they are wearing pajamas," she said. "They sleep with you to-night and to-morrow they go to work with you like mascots."

"How like mascots?" asked the Potato Face Blind Man.

"They are luck bringers. They keep your good luck if it is good. They change your bad luck if it is bad."

"I hear you and my ears get your explanations."

So the next morning when the Potato Face Blind Man sat down to play his accordion on the corner nearest the postoffice in the Village of Liver-and-Onions, next to him on the right hand side sitting on the sidewalk was Poker Face the Baboon and on the left hand side sitting next to him was Hot Dog the Tiger.

They looked like dummies—they were so quiet. They looked as if they were made of wood and paper and then painted. In the eyes of Poker Face was something faraway.

In the eyes of Hot Dog was something hungry. Whitson Whimble, the patent clothes wringer manufacturer, came by in his big limousine automobile car without horses to pull it. He was sitting back on the leather upholstered seat cushions.

"Stop here," he commanded the chauffeur driving the car.

Then Whitson Whimble sat looking. First he looked into the eyes of Poker Face the Baboon and saw something faraway. Then he looked into the eyes of Hot Dog the Tiger and saw something hungry. Then he read the sign painted by the Potato Face Blind Man saying, "You look at 'em and see 'em; I look at 'em and I don't. You watch what their eyes say; I can only feel their hair." Then Whitson Whimble commanded the chauffeur driving the car, "Go on."

Fifteen minutes later a man in overalls came down Main Street with a wheelbarrow. He stopped in front of the Potato Face Blind Man,

Poker Face the Baboon, and Hot Dog the Tiger.

"Where is the aluminum dishpan?" he asked.

"On my left side on the sidewalk," answered the Potato Face Blind Man.

"Where is the galvanized iron washtub?"

"On my right side on the sidewalk."

Then the man in overalls took a shovel and began shoveling silver dollars out of the wheelbarrow into the aluminum dishpan and the galvanized iron washtub. He shoveled out of the wheelbarrow till the dishpan was full, till the washtub was full. Then he put the shovel into the wheelbarrow and went up Main Street.

Six o'clock that night Pick Ups came along. The Potato Face Blind Man said to him, "I have to carry home a heavy load of money tonight, an aluminum dishpan full of silver dollars and a galvanized iron washtub full of silver dollars. So I ask you, will you take care of Poker Face the Baboon and Hot Dog the Tiger?"

"Yes," said Pick Ups, "I will." And he did. He tied a pink string to their legs and took them home and put them in the woodshed.

Poker Face the Baboon went to sleep on the soft coal at the north end of the woodshed and when he was asleep his face had something faraway in it and he was so quiet he looked like a dummy with brown hair of the jungle painted on his black skin and a black nose painted on his brown face. Hot Dog the Tiger went to sleep on the hard coal at the south end of the woodshed and when he was asleep his eyelashes had something hungry in them and he looked like a painted dummy with black stripes painted over his yellow belly and a black spot painted away at the end of his long yellow tail.

In the morning the woodshed was empty. Pick Ups told the Potato Face Blind Man, "They left a note in their own handwriting on perfumed pink paper. It said, '*Mascots never stay long.*'"

And that is why for many years the Potato

Face Blind Man had silver dollars to spend—
and that is why many people in the Rootabaga
Country keep their eyes open for a Watermelon
Moon in the sky with a green rim and red meat
inside and black seeds making spots on the red
meat.

The Toboggan-to-the-Moon Dream of the Potato Face Blind Man

One morning in October the Potato Face Blind Man sat on the corner nearest the post-office.

Any Ice Today came along and said, "This is the sad time of the year."

"Sad?" asked the Potato Face Blind Man, changing his accordion from his right knee to his left knee, and singing softly to the tune he was fumbling on the accordion keys, "Be Happy in the Morning When the Birds Bring the Beans."

"Yes," said Any Ice Today, "is it not sad

every year when the leaves change from green to yellow, when the leaves dry on the branches and fall into the air, and the wind blows them and they make a song saying, 'Hush baby, hush baby,' and the wind fills the sky with them and they are like a sky full of birds who forget they know any songs."

"It is sad and not sad," was the blind man's word.

"Listen," said the Potato Face. "For me this is the time of the year when the dream of the white moon toboggan comes back. Five weeks before the first snow flurry this dream always comes back to me. It says, 'The black leaves are falling now and they fill the sky but five weeks go by and then for every black leaf there will be a thousand snow crystals shining white.'"

"What was your dream of the white moon toboggan?" asked Any Ice Today.

"It came to me first when I was a boy, when I had my eyes, before my luck changed. I saw

60

the big white spiders of the moon working, rushing around climbing up, climbing down, snizzling and sniffering. I looked a long while before I saw what the big white spiders on the moon were doing. I saw after a while they were weaving a long toboggan, a white toboggan, white and soft as snow. And after a long while of snizzling and sniffering, climbing up and climbing down, at last the toboggan was done, a snow white toboggan running from the moon down to the Rootabaga Country.

"And sliding, sliding down from the moon on this toboggan were the White Gold Boys and the Blue Silver Girls. They tumbled down at my feet because, you see, the toboggan ended right at my feet. I could lean over and pick up the White Gold Boys and the Blue Silver Girls as they slid out of the toboggan at my feet. I could pick up a whole handful of them and hold them in my hand and talk with them. Yet, you understand, whenever I tried to shut my hand and keep any of them they would snizzle and sniffer and jump out of the cracks between my fingers. Once there was a little gold and silver dust on my left hand thumb, dust they snizzled out while slipping away from me.

"Once I heard a White Gold Boy and a Blue Silver Girl whispering. They were standing on the tip of my right hand little finger, whispering. One said, 'I got pumpkins—what did you get?' The other said, 'I got hazel nuts.' I listened more and I found out there are millions of pumpkins and millions of hazel nuts so small you and I can not see them. These children from the moon, however, they can see them and whenever they slide down on the moon toboggan they take back their pockets full of things so little we have never seen them."

"They are wonderful children," said Any Ice Today. "And will you tell me how they get back to the moon after they slide down the toboggan?"

"Oh, that is easy," said Potato Face. "It is just as easy for them to slide *up* to the moon as to slide down. Sliding up and sliding down is the same for them. The big white spiders fixed it that way when they snizzled and sniffered and made the toboggan."

How Gimme the Ax Found Out About the Zigzag Railroad and Who Made It Zigzag

One day Gimme the Ax said to himself, "To-day I go to the postoffice and around, looking around. Maybe I will hear about something happening last night when I was sleeping. Maybe a policeman began laughing and fell in a cistern and came out with a wheelbarrow full of goldfish wearing new jewelry. How do I know? Maybe the man in the moon going down a cellar stairs to get a pitcher of butter-milk for the woman in the moon to drink and stop crying, maybe he fell down the stairs and broke the pitcher and laughed and picked up the broken pieces and said to himself, 'One, two, three, four, accidents happen in the best regulated families.' How do I know?"

So with his mind full of simple and refreshing thoughts, Gimme the Ax went out into the backyard garden and looked at the different necktie poppies growing early in the summer. Then he picked one of the necktie poppies to wear for a necktie scarf going downtown to the postoffice and around looking around.

"It is a good speculation to look nice around looking around in a necktie scarf," said Gimme the Ax. "It is a necktie with a picture like whiteface pony spots on a green frog swimming in the moonshine."

So he went downtown. For the first time he saw the Potato Face Blind Man playing an accordion on the corner next nearest the postoffice. He asked the Potato Face to tell him why the railroad tracks run zigzag in the Rootabaga Country.

Found Out About the Zigzag Railroad

"Long ago," said the Potato Face Blind Man, "long before the necktie poppies began growing in the backyard, long before there was a necktie scarf like yours with whiteface pony spots on a green frog swimming in the moonshine, back in the old days when they laid the rails for the railroad they laid the rails straight."

"Then the zizzies came. The zizzy is a bug. He runs zigzag on zigzag legs, eats zigzag with zigzag teeth, and spits zigzag with a zigzag tongue.

"Millions of zizzies came hizzing with little hizzers on their heads and under their legs. They jumped on the rails with their zigzag legs, and spit and twisted with their zigzag teeth and tongues till they twisted the whole railroad and all the rails and tracks into a zigzag railroad with zigzag rails for the trains, the passenger trains and the freight trains, all to run zigzag on.

"Then the zizzies crept away into the fields

67

where they sleep and cover themselves with zigzag blankets on special zigzag beds.

"Next day came shovelmen with their shovels, smooth engineers with smooth blue prints, and water boys with water pails and water dippers for the shovelmen to drink after shoveling the railroad straight. And I nearly forgot to say the steam and hoist operating engineers came and began their steam hoist and operating to make the railroad straight.

"They worked hard. They made the railroad straight again. They looked at the job and said to themselves and to each other, 'This is it—we done it.'

"Next morning the zizzies opened their zigzag eyes and looked over to the railroad and the rails. When they saw the railroad all straight again, and the rails and the ties and the spikes all straight again, the zizzies didn't even eat breakfast that morning.

"They jumped out of their zigzag beds,

jumped onto the rails with their zigzag legs and spit and twisted till they spit and twisted all the rails and the ties and the spikes back into a zigzag like the letter Z and the letter Z at the end of the alphabet.

"After that the zizzies went to breakfast. And they said to themselves and to each other, the same as the shovelmen, the smooth engineers and the steam hoist and operating engineers, 'This is it—we done it.' "

"So that is the how of the which—it was the zizzies," said Gimme the Ax.

"Yes, it was the zizzies," said the Potato Face Blind Man. "That is the story told to me."

"Who told it to you?"

"*Two little zizzies.* They came to me one cold winter night and slept in my accordion where the music keeps it warm in winter. In the morning I said, 'Good morning, zizzies, did you have a good sleep last night and pleasant dreams?' And after they had breakfast they told me the story. Both told it zigzag but it was the same kind of zigzag each had together."

3. Three Stories About the Gold Buckskin Whincher

The Story of Blixie Bimber and the Power of the Gold Buckskin Whincher

Blixie Bimber grew up looking for luck. If she found a horseshoe she took it home and put it on the wall of her room with a ribbon tied to it. She would look at the moon through her fingers, under her arms, over her right shoulder but never—never over her *left* shoulder. She listened and picked up everything anybody said about the ground hog and whether the ground hog saw his shadow when he came out the second of February.

If she dreamed of onions she knew the next day she would find a silver spoon. If she dreamed of fishes she knew the next day she would meet a strange man who would call her by her first name. She grew up looking for luck.

She was sixteen years old and quite a girl, with her skirts down to her shoe tops, when something happened. She was going to the postoffice to see if there was a letter for her from Peter Potato Blossom Wishes, her best chum, or a letter from Jimmy the Flea, her best friend she kept steady company with.

Jimmy the Flea was a climber. He climbed skyscrapers and flagpoles and smokestacks and was a famous steeplejack. Blixie Bimber liked him because he was a steeplejack, a little, but more because he was a whistler.

Every time Blixie said to Jimmy, "I got the blues—whistle the blues out of me," Jimmy would just naturally whistle till the blues just naturally went away from Blixie.

On the way to the postoffice, Blixie found a gold buckskin *whincher*. There it lay in the middle of the sidewalk. How and why it came

74

to be there she never knew and nobody ever told her. "It's luck," she said to herself as she picked it up quick.

And so—she took it home and fixed it on a little chain and wore it around her neck.

She did not know and nobody ever told her a gold buckskin whincher is different from just a plain common whincher. It has a *power*. And if a thing has a power over you then you just naturally can't help yourself.

So—around her neck fixed on a little chain Blixie Bimber wore the gold buckskin whincher and never knew it had a power and all the time the power was working.

"The first man you meet with an X in his name you must fall head over heels in love with him," said the silent power in the gold buckskin whincher.

And that was why Blixie Bimber stopped at the postoffice and went back again asking the clerk at the postoffice window if he was sure there wasn't a letter for her. The name of the clerk was Silas Baxby. For six weeks he kept steady company with Blixie Bimber. They went to dances, hayrack rides, picnics and high jinks together.

All the time the power in the gold buckskin whincher was working. It was hanging by a little chain around her neck and always working. It was saying, "The next man you meet with two X's in his name you must leave all and fall head over heels in love with him."

She met the high school principal. His name was Fritz Axenbax. Blixie dropped her eyes before him and threw smiles at him. And for six weeks he kept steady company with Blixie Bimber. They went to dances, hayrack rides, picnics and high jinks together.

"Why do you go with him for steady company?" her relatives asked.

"It's a power he's got," Blixie answered, "I just can't help it—it's a power."

"One of his feet is bigger than the other—

how can you keep steady company with him?"
they asked again.

All she would answer was, "It's a power."

All the time, of course, the gold buckskin
whincher on the little chain around her neck
was working. It was saying, "If she meets a
man with three X's in his name she must fall
head over heels in love with him."

At a band concert in the public square one
night she met James Sixbixdix. There was
no helping it. She dropped her eyes and threw
her smiles at him. And for six weeks they
kept steady company going to band concerts,
dances, hayrack rides, picnics and high jinks
together.

"Why do you keep steady company with
him? He's a musical soup eater," her relatives said to her. And she answered, "It's a
power—I can't help myself."

Leaning down with her head in a rain water
cistern one day, listening to the echoes against

the strange wooden walls of the cistern, the gold buckskin whincher on the little chain around her neck slipped off and fell down into the rain water.

"My luck is gone," said Blixie. Then she went into the house and made two telephone calls. One was to James Sixbixdix telling him she couldn't keep the date with him that night. The other was to Jimmy the Flea, the climber, the steeplejack.

"Come on over—I got the blues and I want you to whistle 'em away," was what she telephoned Jimmy the Flea.

And so—if you ever come across a gold buckskin whincher, be careful. It's got a power. It'll make you fall head over heels in love with the next man you meet with an X in his name. Or it will do other strange things because different whinchers have different powers.

The Story of Jason Squiff and Why He Had a Popcorn Hat, Popcorn Mittens and Popcorn Shoes

Jason Squiff was a cistern cleaner. He had greenish yellowish hair. If you looked down into a cistern when he was lifting buckets of slush and mud you could tell where he was you could pick him out down in the dark cistern, by the lights of his greenish yellowish hair.

Sometimes the buckets of slush and mud tipped over and ran down on the top of his head. This covered his greenish yellowish hair. And then it was hard to tell where he was and it was not easy to pick him out down in the dark where he was cleaning the cistern.

One day Jason Squiff came to the Bimber house and knocked on the door.

"Did I understand," he said, speaking to Mrs. Bimber, Blixie Bimber's mother, "do I understand you sent for me to clean the cistern in your back yard?"

"You understand exactly such," said Mrs. Bimber, "and you are welcome as the flowers that bloom in the spring, tra-la-la."

"Then I will go to work and clean the cistern, tra-la-la," he answered, speaking to Mrs. Bimber. "I'm the guy, tra-la-la," he said further, running his excellent fingers through his greenish yellowish hair which was shining brightly.

He began cleaning the cistern. Blixie Bimber came out in the back yard. She looked down in the cistern. It was all dark. It looked like nothing but all dark down there. By and by she saw something greenish yellowish. She

80

watched it. Soon she saw it was Jason Squiff's head and hair. And then she knew the cistern was being cleaned and Jason Squiff was on the job. So she sang tra-la-la and went back into the house and told her mother Jason Squiff was on the job.

The last bucketful of slush and mud came at last for Jason Squiff. He squinted at the bottom. Something was shining. He reached his fingers down through the slush and mud and took out what was shining.

It was the gold buckskin whincher Blixie Bimber lost from the gold chain around her neck the week before when she was looking down into the cistern to see what she could see. It was exactly the same gold buckskin whincher shining and glittering like a sign of happiness.

"It's luck," said Jason Squiff, wiping his fingers on his greenish yellowish hair. Then he put the gold buckskin whincher in his vest pocket and spoke to himself again, "It's luck."

A little after six o'clock that night Jason

Squiff stepped into his house and home and said hello to his wife and daughters. They all began to laugh. Their laughter was a ticklish laughter.

"Something funny is happening," he said.

"And you are it," they all laughed at him again with ticklish laughter.

Then they showed him. His hat was popcorn, his mittens popcorn and his shoes popcorn. He didn't know the gold buckskin whincher had a power and was working all the time. He didn't know the whincher in his vest pocket was saying, "You have a letter Q in your name and because you have the pleasure and happiness of having a Q in your name you must have a popcorn hat, popcorn mittens and popcorn shoes."

The next morning he put on another hat, another pair of mittens and another pair of shoes. And the minute he put them on they changed to popcorn.

So he tried on all his hats, mittens and shoes.

His hat was popcorn, his mittens popcorn and his shoes popcorn

Always they changed to popcorn the minute he had them on.

He went downtown to the stores. He bought a new hat, mittens and shoes. And the minute he had them on they changed to popcorn.

So he decided he would go to work and clean cisterns with his popcorn hat, popcorn mittens and popcorn shoes on.

The people of the Village of Cream Puffs enjoyed watching him walk up the street, going to clean cisterns. People five and six blocks away could see him coming and going with his popcorn hat, popcorn mittens and popcorn shoes.

When he was down in a cistern the children enjoyed looking down into the cistern to see him work. When none of the slush and mud fell on his hat and mittens he was easy to find. The light of the shining popcorn lit up the whole inside of the cistern.

Sometimes, of course, the white popcorn got

full of black slush and black mud. And then when Jason Squiff came up and walked home he was not quite so dazzling to look at.

It was a funny winter for Jason Squiff.

"It's a crime, a dirty crime," he said to himself. "Now I can never be alone with my thoughts. Everybody looks at me when I go up the street."

"If I meet a funeral even the pall bearers begin to laugh at my popcorn hat. If I meet people going to a wedding they throw all the rice at me as if I am a bride and a groom all together.

"The horses try to eat my hat wherever I go. Three hats I have fed to horses this winter.

"And if I accidentally drop one of my mittens the chickens eat it."

Then Jason Squiff began to change. He became proud.

"I always wanted a white beautiful hat like this white popcorn hat," he said to himself.

86

"And I always wanted white beautiful mittens and white beautiful shoes like these white popcorn mittens and shoes."

When the boys yelled, "Snow man! yah-de-dah-de-dah, Snow man!" he just waved his hand to them with an upward gesture of his arm to show he was proud of how he looked.

"They all watch for me," he said to himself, "I am distinquished—am I not?" he asked himself.

And he put his right hand into his left hand and shook hands with himself and said, "You certainly look fixed up."

One day he decided to throw away his vest. In the vest pocket was the gold buckskin whincher, with the power working, the power saying, "You have a letter Q in your name and because you have the pleasure and happiness of having a Q in your name you must have a popcorn hat, popcorn mittens and popcorn shoes."

Yes, he threw away the vest. He forgot all about the gold buckskin whincher being in the vest.

He just handed the vest to a rag man. And the rag man put the vest with the gold buckskin whincher in a bag on his back and walked away.

After that Jason Squiff was like other people. His hats would never change to popcorn nor his mittens to popcorn nor his shoes to popcorn.

And when anybody looked at him down in a cistern cleaning the cistern or when anybody saw him walking along the street they knew him by his greenish yellowish hair which was always full of bright lights.

And so—if you have a Q in your name, be careful if you ever come across a gold buckskin whincher. Remember different whinchers have different powers.

The Story of Rags Habakuk, the Two Blue Rats, and the Circus Man Who Came with Spot Cash Money

Rags Habakuk was going home. His day's work was done. The sun was down. Street lamps began shining. Burglars were starting on their night's work. It was no time for an honest ragman to be knocking on people's back doors, saying, "Any rags?" or else saying, "Any rags? any bottles? any bones?" or else saying "Any rags? any bottles? any bones? any old iron? any copper, brass, old shoes all run down and no good to anybody to-day? any old clothes, old coats, pants, vests? I take any old clothes you got."

Yes, Rags Habakuk was going home. In the gunnysack bag on his back, humped up on top of the rag humps in the bag, was an old vest. It was the same old vest Jason Squiff threw out of a door at Rags Habakuk. In the pocket of the vest was the gold buckskin whincher with a power in it.

Well, Rags Habakuk got home just like always, sat down to supper and smacked his mouth and had a big supper of fish, just like always. Then he went out to a shanty in the back yard and opened up the gunnysack rag bag and fixed things out classified just like every day when he came home he opened the gunnysack bag and fixed things out classified.

The last thing of all he fixed out classified was the vest with the gold buckskin whincher in the pocket. "Put it on—it's a glad rag," he said, looking at the vest. "It's a lucky vest." So he put his right arm in the right armhole and his left arm in the left armhole. And there he was with his arms in the armholes of the old vest all fixed out classified new.

Next morning Rags Habakuk kissed his wife g'by and his eighteen year old girl g'by and his nineteen year old girl g'by. He kissed them just like he always kissed them—in a hurry—and as he kissed each one he said, "I will be back soon if not sooner and when I come back I will return."

Yes, up the street went Rags Habakuk. And soon as he left home something happened. Standing on his right shoulder was a blue rat and standing on his left shoulder was a blue rat. The only way he knew they were there was by looking at them.

There they were, close to his ears. He could feel the far edge of their whiskers against his ears.

"This never happened to me before all the time I been picking rags," he said. "Two blue rats stand by my ears and never say anything even if they know I am listening to anything they tell me."

So Rags Habakuk walked on two blocks, three blocks, four blocks, squinting with his right eye slanting at the blue rat on his right shoulder and squinting with his left eye slanting at the blue rat on his left shoulder.

"If I stood on somebody's shoulder with my whiskers right up in somebody's ear I would say something for somebody to listen to," he muttered.

Of course, he did not understand it was the gold buckskin whincher and the power working. Down in the pocket of the vest he had on, the gold buckskin whincher power was saying, "Because you have two K's in your name you must have two blue rats on your shoulders, one blue rat for your right ear, one blue rat for your left ear."

It was good business. Never before did Rags Habakuk get so much old rags.

Blue Rats and the Circus Man

"Come again—you and your lucky blue rats," people said to him. They dug into their cellars and garrets and brought him bottles and bones and copper and brass and old shoes and old clothes, coats, pants, vests.

Every morning when he went up the street with the two blue rats on his shoulders, blinking their eyes straight ahead and chewing their whiskers so they sometimes tickled the ears of old Rags Habakuk, sometimes women came running out on the front porch to look at him and say, "Well, if he isn't a queer old mysterious ragman and if those ain't queer old mysterious blue rats!"

All the time the gold buckskin whincher and the power was working. It was saying, "So long as old Rags Habakuk keeps the two blue rats he shall have good luck—but if he ever sells one of the blue rats then one of his daughters shall marry a taxicab driver—and if he ever sells the other blue rat then his other daughter shall marry a moving-picture hero actor."

Then terrible things happened. A circus man came. "I give you one thousand dollars spot cash money for one of the blue rats," he expostulated with his mouth. "And I give you two thousand dollars spot cash money for the two of the blue rats both of them together."

"Show me how much spot cash money two thousand dollars is all counted out in one pile for one man to carry away home in his gunny-sack rag bag," was the answer of Rags Habakuk.

The circus man went to the bank and came back with spot cash greenbacks money.

"This spot cash greenbacks money is made from the finest silk rags printed by the national government for the national republic to make business rich and prosperous," said the circus man, expostulating with his mouth.

"T-h-e f-i-n-e-s-t s-i-l-k r-a-g-s," he expostulated again holding two fingers under the nose of Rags Habakuk.

"I take it," said Rags Habakuk, "I take it. It is a whole gunnysack bag full of spot cash greenbacks money. I tell my wife it is printed by the national government for the national republic to make business rich and prosperous."

Then he kissed the blue rats, one on the right ear, the other on the left ear, and handed them over to the circus man.

And that was why the next month his eighteen year old daughter married a taxicab driver who was so polite all the time to his customers that he never had time to be polite to his wife.

And that was why his nineteen year old daughter married a moving-picture hero actor who worked so hard being nice and kind in the moving pictures that he never had enough left over for his wife when he got home after the day's work.

The Story of Rags Habakuk

And the lucky vest with the gold buckskin whincher was stolen from Rags Habakuk by the taxicab driver.

4. Four Stories About the Deep Doom of Dark Doorways

People: The Rag Doll
The Broom Handle
Spoon Lickers
Chocolate Chins
Dirty Bibs
Tin Pan Bangers
Clean Ears
Easy Ticklers
Musical Soup Eaters
Chubby Chubs
Sleepy Heads

Snoo Foo
Blink, Swink and Jink
Blunk, Swunk and Junk
Missus Sniggers

Eeta Peeca Pie
Meeny Miney
Miney Mo
A Potato Bug Millionaire

Bimbo the Snip
Bevo the Hike
A Ward Alderman
A Barn Boss
A Weather Man
A Traffic Policeman
A Monkey
A Widow Woman
An Umbrella Handle Maker

The Wedding Procession of the Rag Doll and the Broom Handle and Who Was in It

The Rag Doll had many friends. The Whisk Broom, the Furnace Shovel, the Coffee Pot, they all liked the Rag Doll very much.

But when the Rag Doll married, it was the Broom Handle she picked because the Broom Handle fixed her eyes.

A proud child, proud but careless, banged the head of the Rag Doll against a door one day and knocked off both the glass eyes sewed on long ago. It was then the Broom Handle found two black California prunes, and fastened the two California prunes just where the eyes belonged. So then the Rag Doll had two fine black eyes brand new. She was even nicknamed Black Eyes by some people.

There was a wedding when the Rag Doll married the Broom Handle. It was a grand wedding with one of the grandest processions ever seen at a rag doll wedding. And we are sure no broom handle ever had a grander wedding procession when he got married.

Who marched in the procession? Well, first came the Spoon Lickers. Every one of them had a tea spoon, or a soup spoon, though most of them had a big table spoon. On the spoons, what did they have? Oh, some had butter scotch, some had gravy, some had marshmallow fudge. Every one had something slickery sweet or fat to eat on the spoon. And as they marched in the wedding procession of the Rag Doll and the Broom Handle, they licked their spoons and looked around and licked their spoons again.

Next came the Tin Pan Bangers. Some had dishpans, some had frying pans, some had potato peeling pans. All the pans were tin with tight tin bottoms. And the Tin Pan Bangers banged with knives and forks and iron and wooden bangers on the bottoms of the tin pans. And as they marched in the wedding procession of the Rag Doll and the Broom Handle they banged their pans and looked around and banged again.

Then came the Chocolate Chins. They were all eating chocolates. And the chocolate was slippery and slickered all over their chins. Some of them spattered the ends of their noses with black chocolate. Some of them spread the brown chocolate nearly up to their ears. And then as they marched in the wedding procession of the Rag Doll and the Broom Handle they stuck their chins in the air and looked around and stuck their chins in the air again.

Then came the Dirty Bibs. They wore plain

white bibs, checker bibs, stripe bibs, blue bibs and bibs with butterflies. But all the bibs were dirty. The plain white bibs were dirty, the checker bibs were dirty, the stripe bibs, the blue bibs and the bibs with butterflies on them, they were all dirty. And so in the wedding procession of the Rag Doll and the Broom Handle, the Dirty Bibs marched with their dirty fingers on the bibs and they looked around and laughed and looked around and laughed again.

Next came the Clean Ears. They were proud. How they got into the procession nobody knows. Their ears were all clean. They were clean not only on the outside but they were clean on the inside. There was not a speck of dirt or dust or muss or mess on the inside nor the outside of their ears. And so in the wedding procession of the Rag Doll and the Broom Handle, they wiggled their ears and looked around and wiggled their ears again.

The Easy Ticklers were next in the procession. Their faces were shining. Their cheeks

And Broom Handle and Who Was in It

were like bars of new soap. Their ribs were strong and the meat and the fat was thick on their ribs. It was plain to see they were saying, "Don't tickle me because I tickle so easy." And as they marched in the wedding procession of the Rag Doll and the Broom Handle, they tickled themselves and laughed and looked around and tickled themselves again.

The music was furnished mostly by the Musical Soup Eaters. They marched with big bowls of soup in front of them and big spoons for eating the soup. They whistled and chuzzled and snozzled the soup and the noise they made could be heard far up at the head of the procession where the Spoon Lickers were marching. So they dipped their soup and looked around and dipped their soup again.

The Chubby Chubs were next. They were roly poly, round faced smackers and snoozers. They were not fat babies—oh no, oh no—not fat but just chubby and easy to squeeze. They marched on their chubby legs and chubby feet and chubbed their chubbs and looked around and chubbed their chubbs again.

The last of all in the wedding procession of the Rag Doll and the Broom Handle were the Sleepyheads. They were smiling and glad to be marching but their heads were slimpsing down and their smiles were half fading away and their eyes were half shut or a little more than half shut. They staggered just a little as though their feet were not sure where they were going. They were the Sleepyheads, the last of all, in the wedding procession of the Rag Doll and the Broom Handle and the Sleepyheads they never looked around at all.

It *was* a grand procession, don't you think so?

How the Hat Ashes Shovel Helped Snoo Foo

If you want to remember the names of all six of the Sniggers children, remember that the three biggest were named Blink, Swink and Jink but the three littlest ones were named Blunk, Swunk and Junk. One day last January the three biggest had a fuss with the three littlest. The fuss was about a new hat for Snoo Foo, the snow man, about what kind of a hat he should wear and how he should wear it. Blink, Swink and Jink said, "He wants a crooked hat put on straight." Blunk, Swunk and Junk said, "He wants a straight hat put on crooked." They fussed and fussed. Blink fussed with Blunk, Swink fussed with Swunk, and Jink fussed with Junk. The first ones to make up after the fuss were Jink and Junk. They decided the best way to settle the fuss. "Let's put a crooked hat on crooked," said Jink. "No, let's put a straight hat on straight," said Junk. Then they stood looking and looking into each other's shiny laughing eyes and then both of them exploded to each other at the same time, "Let's put on two hats, a crooked hat crooked and a straight hat straight."

Well, they looked around for hats. But there were not any hats anywhere, that is, no hats big enough for a snow man with a big head like Snoo Foo. So they went in the house and asked their mother for *the hat ashes shovel*. Of course, in most any other house, the mother would be all worried if six children came tramping and clomping in, banging the door and all six ejaculating to their mother at once, "Where is the hat ashes shovel?" But Missus Sniggers wasn't worried at all. She rubbed her chin with her finger and said softly, "Oh lah de dah, oh lah de dah, where is that hat ashes shovel, last week I had it when I was making a hat for Mister Sniggers; I remember I had that hat ashes shovel right up here over the clock, oh lah de dah, oh lah de dah. Go out and ring the front door bell," she said to Jink Sniggers. Jink ran away to the front door. And Missus Sniggers and the five children waited. Bling-bling the bell began ringing and—listen —the door of the clock opened and the hat ashes shovel fell out. "Oh lah de dah, get out of here in a hurry," said Missus Sniggers.

Well, the children ran out and dug a big pail of hat ashes with the hat ashes shovel. And they made two hats for Snoo Foo. One was a crooked hat. The other was a straight hat. And they put the crooked hat on crooked and the straight hat on straight. And there stood

107

How Snoo Foo Was Helped

Snoo Foo in the front yard and everybody who came by on the street, he would take off his hat to them, the crooked hat with his arm crooked and the straight hat with his arm straight. That was the end of the fuss between the Sniggers children and it was Jink, the littlest one of the biggest, and Junk, the littlest one of the littlest, who settled the fuss by looking clean into each other's eyes and laughing. If you ever get into a fuss try this way of settling it.

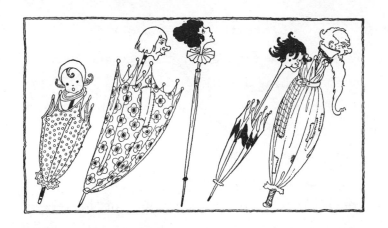

Three Boys With Jugs of Molasses and Secret Ambitions

In the Village of Liver-and-Onions, if *one* boy goes to the grocery for a jug of molasses it is just like always. And if *two* boys go to the grocery for a jug of molasses together it is just like always. But if *three* boys go to the grocery for a jug of molasses each and all together then it is not like always at all, at all.

Eeta Peeca Pie grew up with wishes and wishes working inside him. And for every wish inside him he had a freckle outside on his face. Whenever he smiled the smile ran way back into the far side of his face and got lost in the wishing freckles.

Meeny Miney grew up with suspicions and suspicions working inside him. And after a while some of the suspicions got fastened on his eyes and some of the suspicions got fastened on his mouth. So when he looked at other people straight in the face they used to say, "Meeny Miney looks so sad-like I wonder if he'll get by."

Miney Mo was different. He wasn't sad-like and suspicious like Meeny Miney. Nor was he full of wishes inside and freckles outside like Eeta Peeca Pie. He was all mixed up inside with wishes and suspicions. So he had a few freckles and a few suspicions on his face. When he looked other people straight in the face they used to say, "I don't know whether to laugh or cry."

So here we have 'em, three boys growing up with wishes, suspicions and mixed-up wishes and suspicions. They all looked different from each other. Each one, however, had a secret ambition. And all three had the same secret ambition.

An ambition is a little creeper that creeps and creeps in your heart night and day, singing a little song, "Come and find me, come and find me."

The secret ambition in the heart of Eeta Peeca Pie, Meeney Miney, and Miney Mo was an ambition to go railroading, to ride on railroad cars night and day, year after year. The whistles and the wheels of railroad trains were music to them.

Whenever the secret ambition crept in their hearts and made them too sad, so sad it was hard to live and stand for it, they would all three put their hands on each other's shoulder and sing the song of Joe. The chorus was like this:

> Joe, Joe, broke his toe,
> On the way to Mexico.
> Came back, broke his back,
> Sliding on the railroad track.

One fine summer morning all three mothers of all three boys gave each one a jug and said, "Go to the grocery and get a jug of molasses." All three got to the grocery at the same time. And all three went out of the door of the grocery together, each with a jug of molasses together and each with his secret ambition creeping around in his heart, all three together.

Two blocks from the grocery they stopped under a slippery elm tree. Eeta Peeca Pie was stretching his neck looking straight up into the slippery elm tree. He said it was always good for his freckles and it helped his wishes to stand under a slippery elm and look up.

While he was looking up his left hand let go the jug handle of the jug of molasses. And the jug went ka-flump, ka-flumpety-flump down on the stone sidewalk, cracked to pieces and let the molasses go running out over the sidewalk.

If you have never seen it, let me tell you molasses running out of a broken jug, over a stone

They stepped into the molasses with their bare feet

sidewalk under a slippery elm tree, looks peculiar and mysterious.

Eeta Peeca Pie stepped into the molasses with his bare feet. "It's a lotta fun," he said. "It tickles all over." So Meeney Miney and Miney Mo both stepped into the molasses with their bare feet.

Then what happened just happened. One got littler. Another got littler. All three got littler.

"You look to me only big as a potato bug," said Eeta Peeca Pie to Meeney Miney and Miney Mo. "It's the same like you look to us," said Meeney Miney and Miney Mo to Eeta Peeca Pie. And then because their secret ambition began to hurt them they all stood with hands on each other's shoulders and sang the Mexico Joe song.

Off the sidewalk they strolled, across a field of grass. They passed many houses of spiders and ants. In front of one house they saw Mrs.

Spider over a tub washing clothes for Mr. Spider.

"Why do you wear that frying pan on your head?" they asked her.

"In this country all ladies wear the frying pan on their head when they want a hat."

"But what if you want a hat when you are frying with the frying pan?" asked Eeta Peeca Pie.

"That never happens to any respectable lady in this country."

"Don't you never have no new style hats?" asked Meeney Miney.

"No, but we always have new style frying pans every spring and fall."

Hidden in the roots of a pink grass clump, they came to a city of twisted-nose spiders. On the main street was a store with a show window full of pink parasols. They walked in and said to the clerk, "We want to buy parasols."

"We don't sell parasols here," said the spider clerk.

"Well, lend us a parasol apiece," said all three.

"Gladly, most gladly," said the clerk.

"How do you do it?" asked Eeta.

"I don't have to," answered the spider clerk.

"How did it begin?"

"It never was otherwise."

"Don't you never get tired?"

"Every parasol is a joy."

"What do you do when the parasols are gone?"

"They always come back. These are the famous twisted-nose parasols made from the famous pink grass. You will lose them all, all three. Then they will all walk back to me here in this store on main street. I can not sell you something I know you will surely lose. Neither can I ask you to pay, for something you will forget, somewhere sometime, and when you forget it, it will walk back here to me again. Look—look!"

As he said "Look," the door opened and five

pink parasols came waltzing in and waltzed up into the show window.

"They always come back. Everybody forgets. Take your parasols and go. You will forget them and they will come back to me."

"He looks like he had wishes inside him," said Eeta Peeca Pie.

"He looks like he had suspicions," said Meeney Miney.

"He looks like he was all mixed up wishes and suspicions," said Miney Mo.

And once more because they all felt lonesome and their secret ambitions were creeping and eating, they put their hands on their shoulders and sang the Mexico Joe song.

Then came happiness. They entered the Potato Bug Country. And they had luck first of all the first hour they were in the Potato Bug Country. They met a Potato Bug millionaire.

"How are you a millionaire?" they asked him.

"Because I got a million," he answered.

"A million what?"

"A million *fleems*."

"Who wants fleems?"

"You want fleems if you're going to live here."

"Why so?"

"Because fleems is our money. In the Potato Bug Country, if you got no fleems you can't buy nothing nor anything. But if you got a million fleems you're a Potato Bug millionaire."

Then he surprised them.

"I like you because you got wishes and freckles," he said to Eeta Peeca Pie, filling the pockets of Eeta with fleems.

"And I like you because you got suspicions and you're sad-like," he said to Meeney Miney filling Meeney Miney's pockets full of fleems.

"And I like you because you got some wishes and some suspicions and you look mixed up," he said to Miney Mo, sticking handfuls and handfuls of fleems into the pockets of Miney Mo.

Wishes do come true. And suspicions do come true. Here they had been wishing all their lives, and had suspicions of what was going to happen, and now it all came true.

With their pockets filled with fleems they rode on all the railroad trains of the Potato Bug Country. They went to the railroad stations and bought tickets for the fast trains and the slow trains and even the trains that back up and run backward instead of where they start to go.

On the dining cars of the railroads of the Potato Bug Country they ate wonder ham from the famous Potato Bug Pigs, eggs from the Potato Bug Hens, et cetera.

It seemed to them they stayed a long while in the Potato Bug Country, years and years. Yes, the time came when all their fleems were gone. Then whenever they wanted a railroad ride or something to eat or a place to sleep, they put their hands on each other's shoulders and sang the Mexico Joe song. In the Potato Bug

Country they all said the Mexico Joe song was wonderful.

One morning while they were waiting to take an express train on the Early Ohio & Southwestern they sat near the roots of a big potato plant under the big green leaves. And far above them they saw a dim black cloud and they heard a shaking and a rustling and a spattering. They did not know it was a man of the Village of Liver-and-Onions. They did not know it was Mr. Sniggers putting paris green on the potato plants.

A big drop of paris green spattered down and fell onto the heads and shoulders of all three, Eeta Peeca Pie, Meeny Miney and Miney Mo.

Then what happened just happened. They got bigger and bigger—one, two, three. And when they jumped up and ran out of the potato rows, Mr. Sniggers thought they were boys playing tricks.

When they got home to their mothers and told all about the jug of molasses breaking on the stone sidewalk under the slippery elm tree, their mothers said it was careless. The boys said it was lucky because it helped them get their secret ambitions.

And a secret ambition is a little creeper that creeps and creeps in your heart night and day, singing a little song, "Come and find me, come and find me."

How Bimbo the Snip's Thumb Stuck to His Nose When the Wind Changed

Once there was a boy in the Village of Liver-and-Onions whose name was Bimbo the Snip. He forgot nearly everything his father and mother told him to do and told him not to do.

One day his father, Bevo the Hike, came home and found Bimbo the Snip sitting on the front steps with his thumb fastened to his nose and the fingers wiggling.

"I can't take my thumb away," said Bimbo the Snip, "because when I put my thumb to my nose and wiggled my fingers at the iceman the

How Bimbo the Snip's Thumb Stuck to

wind changed. And just like mother always
said, if the wind changed the thumb would stay
fastened to my nose and not come off."

Bevo the Hike took hold of the thumb and
pulled. He tied a clothes line rope around it
and pulled. He pushed with his foot and heel
against it. And all the time the thumb stuck
fast and the fingers wiggled from the end of
the nose of Bimbo the Snip.

Bevo the Hike sent for the ward alderman.
The ward alderman sent for the barn boss of
the street cleaning department. The barn boss
of the street cleaning department sent for the
head vaccinator of the vaccination bureau of the
health department. The head vaccinator of the
vaccination bureau of the health department
sent for the big main fixer of the weather bureau where they understand the tricks of the
wind and the wind changing.

And the big main fixer of the weather bureau said, "If you hit the thumb six times with

124

the end of a traffic policeman's club, the thumb will come loose."

So Bevo the Hike went to a traffic policeman standing on a street corner with a whistle telling the wagons and cars which way to go.

He told the traffic policeman, "The wind changed and Bimbo the Snip's thumb is fastened to his nose and will not come loose till it is hit six times with the end of a traffic policeman's club."

"I can't help you unless you find a monkey to take my place standing on the corner telling the wagons and cars which way to go," answered the traffic policeman.

So Bevo the Hike went to the zoo and said to a monkey, "The wind changed and Bimbo the Snip's thumb is fastened to his nose and will not come loose till it is hit with the end of a traffic policeman's club six times and the traffic policeman cannot leave his place on the street corner telling the traffic which way to go unless a monkey comes and takes his place."

The monkey answered, "Get me a ladder with a whistle so I can climb up and whistle and tell the traffic which way to go."

So Bevo the Hike hunted and hunted over the city and looked and looked and asked and asked till his feet and his eyes and his head and his heart were tired from top to bottom.

Then he met an old widow woman whose husband had been killed in a sewer explosion when he was digging sewer ditches. And the old woman was carrying a bundle of picked-up kindling wood in a bag on her back because she did not have money enough to buy coal.

Bevo the Hike told her, "You have troubles. So have I. You are carrying a load on your back people can see. I am carrying a load and nobody sees it."

"Tell me your troubles," said the old widow woman. He told her. And she said, "In the next block is an old umbrella handle maker.

His Nose When the Wind Changed

He has a ladder with a whistle. He climbs on the ladder when he makes long long umbrella handles. And he has the whistle on the ladder to be whistling."

Bevo the Hike went to the next block, found the house of the umbrella handle maker and said to him, "The wind changed and Bimbo the Snip's thumb is fastened to his nose and will not come loose till it is hit with the end of a traffic policeman's club six times and the traffic policeman cannot leave the corner where he is telling the traffic which way to go unless a monkey takes his place and the monkey cannot take his place unless he has a ladder with a whistle to stand on and whistle the wagons and cars which way to go."

Then the umbrella handle maker said, "To-night I have a special job because I must work on a long, long umbrella handle and I will need the ladder to climb up and the whistle to be whistling. But if you promise to have the ladder back by to-night you can take it."

Bimbo the Snip's Thumb

Bevo the Hike promised. Then he took the ladder with a whistle to the monkey, the monkey took the place of the traffic policeman while the traffic policeman went to the home of Bevo the Hike where Bimbo the Snip was sitting on the front steps with his thumb fastened to his nose wiggling his fingers at everybody passing by on the street.

The traffic policeman hit Bimbo the Snip's thumb five times with the club. And the thumb stuck fast. But the sixth time it was hit with the end of the traffic policeman's thumb club, it came loose.

Then Bevo thanked the policeman, thanked the monkey, and took the ladder with the whistle back to the umbrella handle maker's house and thanked him.

When Bevo the Hike got home that night Bimbo the Snip was in bed and all tickled. He said to his father, "I will be careful how I stick my thumb to my nose and wiggle my fingers the next time the wind changes."

The monkey took the place of the traffic policeman

5. Three Stories About Three Ways the Wind Went Winding

People: Two Skyscrapers
The Northwest Wind
The Golden Spike Limited Train
A Tin Brass Goat
A Tin Brass Goose
Newsies

Young Leather
Red Slippers
A Man to be Hanged
Five Jackrabbits

The Wooden Indian
The Shaghorn Buffalo
The Night Policeman

The Two Skyscrapers Who Decided to Have a Child

Two skyscrapers stood across the street from each other in the Village of Liver-and-Onions. In the daylight when the streets poured full of people buying and selling, these two skyscrapers talked with each other the same as mountains talk.

In the night time when all the people buying and selling were gone home and there were only policemen and taxicab drivers on the streets, in the night when a mist crept up the streets and threw a purple and gray wrapper over everything, in the night when the stars and the sky shook out sheets of purple and gray mist down over the town, then the two skyscrapers leaned toward each other and whispered.

Whether they whispered secrets to each other or whether they whispered simple things that you and I know and everybody knows, that is their secret. One thing is sure: they often were seen leaning toward each other and whispering in the night the same as mountains lean and whisper in the night.

High on the roof of one of the skyscrapers was a tin brass goat looking out across prairies, and silver blue lakes shining like blue porcelain breakfast plates, and out across silver snakes of winding rivers in the morning sun. And high on the roof of the other skyscraper was a tin brass goose looking out across prairies, and silver blue lakes shining like blue porcelain breakfast plates, and out across silver snakes of winding rivers in the morning sun.

Decided to Have a Child

Now the Northwest Wind was a friend of the two skyscrapers. Coming so far, coming five hundred miles in a few hours, coming so fast always while the skyscrapers were standing still, standing always on the same old street corners always, the Northwest Wind was a bringer of news.

"Well, I see the city is here yet," the Northwest Wind would whistle to the skyscrapers.

And they would answer, "Yes, and are the mountains standing yet way out yonder where you come from, Wind?"

"Yes, the mountains are there yonder, and farther yonder is the sea, and the railroads are still going, still running across the prairie to the mountains, to the sea," the Northwest Wind would answer.

And now there was a pledge made by the Northwest Wind to the two skyscrapers. Often the Northwest Wind shook the tin brass goat and shook the tin brass goose on top of the skyscrapers.

"Are you going to blow loose the tin brass goat on my roof?" one asked.

"Are you going to blow loose the tin brass goose on my roof?" the other asked.

"Oh, no," the Northwest Wind laughed, first to one and then to the other, "if I ever blow loose your tin brass goat and if I ever blow loose your tin brass goose, it will be when I am sorry for you because you are up against hard luck and there is somebody's funeral."

So time passed on and the two skyscrapers stood with their feet among the policemen and the taxicabs, the people buying and selling, —the customers with parcels, packages and bundles—while away high on their roofs stood the goat and the goose looking out on silver blue lakes like blue porcelain breakfast plates and silver snakes of rivers winding in the morning sun.

So time passed on and the Northwest Wind kept coming, telling the news and making promises.

Decided to Have a Child

So time passed on. And the two skyscrapers decided to have a child.

And they decided when their child came it should be a *free* child.

"It must be a free child," they said to each other. "It must not be a child standing still all its life on a street corner. Yes, if we have a child she must be free to run across the prairie, to the mountains, to the sea. Yes, it must be a free child."

So time passed on. Their child came. It was a railroad train, the Golden Spike Limited, the fastest long distance train in the Rootabaga Country. It ran across the prairie, to the mountains, to the sea.

They were glad, the two skyscrapers were, glad to have a free child running away from the big city, far away to the mountains, far away to the sea, running as far as the farthest mountains and sea coasts touched by the Northwest Wind.

They were glad their child was useful, the

137

two skyscrapers were, glad their child was carrying a thousand people a thousand miles a day, so when people spoke of the Golden Spike Limited, they spoke of it as a strong, lovely child.

Then time passed on. There came a day when the newsies yelled as though they were crazy. "Yah yah, blah blah, yoh yoh," was what it sounded like to the two skyscrapers who never bothered much about what the newsies were yelling.

"Yah yah, blah blah, yoh yoh," was the cry of the newsies that came up again to the tops of the skyscrapers.

At last the yelling of the newsies came so strong the skyscrapers listened and heard the newsies yammering, "All about the great train wreck! All about the Golden Spike disaster! Many lives lost! Many lives lost!"

And the Northwest Wind came howling a slow sad song. And late that afternoon a crowd of policemen, taxicab drivers, newsies and customers with bundles, all stood around talking and wondering about two things next to each other on the street car track in the middle of the street. One was a tin brass goat. The other was a tin brass goose. And they lay next to each other.

The Dollar Watch and the Five Jack Rabbits

Long ago, long before the waylacks lost the wonderful stripes of oat straw gold and the spots of timothy hay green in their marvelous curving tail feathers, long before the doo-doo-jangers whistled among the honeysuckle blossoms and the bitter-basters cried their last and dying wrangling cries, long before the sad happenings that came later, it was then, some years earlier than the year Fifty Fifty, that Young Leather and Red Slippers crossed the Rootabaga Country.

To begin with, they were walking across the Rootabaga Country. And they were walking because it made their feet glad to feel the dirt of the earth under their shoes and they were close to the smells of the earth. They learned the ways of birds and bugs, why birds have wings, why bugs have legs, why the gladdy-whingers have spotted eggs in a basket nest in a booblow tree, and why the chizzywhizzies scrape off little fiddle songs all summer long while the summer nights last.

Early one morning they were walking across the corn belt of the Rootabaga Country singing, "Deep Down Among the Dagger Dancers." They had just had a breakfast of coffee and hot hankypank cakes covered with cow's butter. Young Leather said to Red Slippers, "What is the best secret we have come across this summer?"

"That is easy to answer," Red Slippers said with a long flish of her long black eyelashes. "The best secret we have come across is a rope of gold hanging from every star in the sky and when we want to go up we go up."

Walking on they came to a town where they met a man with a sorry face. "Why?" they asked him. And he answered, "My brother is in jail."

"What for?" they asked him again. And he answered again, "My brother put on a straw hat in the middle of the winter and went out on the streets laughing; my brother had his hair cut pompompadour and went out on the streets bareheaded in the summertime laughing; and these things were against the law. Worst of all he sneezed at the wrong time and he sneezed before the wrong persons; he sneezed when it was not wise to sneeze. So he will be hanged to-morrow morning. The gallows made of lumber and the rope made of hemp —they are waiting for him to-morrow morning. They will tie around his neck the hangman's necktie and hoist him high."

The man with a sorry face looked more sorry

than ever. It made Young Leather feel reckless and it made Red Slippers feel reckless. They whispered to each other. Then Young Leather said, "Take this dollar watch. Give it to your brother. Tell him when they are leading him to the gallows he must take this dollar watch in his hand, wind it up and push on the stem winder. The rest will be easy."

So the next morning when they were leading the man to be hanged to the gallows made of lumber and the rope made of hemp, where they were going to hoist him high because he sneezed in the wrong place before the wrong people, he used his fingers winding up the watch and pushing on the stem winder. There was a snapping and a slatching like a gas engine slipping into a big pair of dragon fly wings. The dollar watch changed into a dragon fly ship. The man who was going to be hanged jumped into the dragon fly ship and flew whonging away before anybody could stop him.

The Five Jack Rabbits

Young Leather and Red Slippers were walking out of the town laughing and singing again, "Deep Down Among the Dagger Dancers." The man with a sorry face, not so sorry now any more, came running after them. Behind the man and running after him were five long-legged spider jack-rabbits.

"These are for you," was his exclamation. And they all sat down on the stump of a boo-blow tree. He opened his sorry face and told the secrets of the five long-legged spider jack-rabbits to Young Leather and Red Slippers. They waved good-by and went on up the road leading the five new jack-rabbits.

In the next town they came to was a sky-scraper higher than all the other skyscrapers. A rich man dying wanted to be remembered and left in his last will and testament a command they should build a building so high it would scrape the thunder clouds and stand higher than all other skyscrapers with his name carved in stone letters on the top of it, and an electric sign at night with his name on it, and a clock on the tower with his name on it.

"I am hungry to be remembered and have my name spoken by many people after I am dead," the rich man told his friends. "I command you, therefore, to throw the building high in the air because the higher it goes the longer I will be remembered and the longer the years men will mention my name after I am dead."

So there it was. Young Leather and Red Slippers laughed when they first saw the skyscraper, when they were far off along a country road singing their old song, "Deep Down Among the Dagger Dancers."

"We got a show and we give a performance and we want the whole town to see it," was what Young Leather and Red Slippers said to the mayor of the town when they called on him at the city hall. "We want a license and a permit to give this free show in the public square."

"What do you do?" asked the mayor.

The Five Jack Rabbits

"We jump five jack-rabbits, five long-legged spider jack-rabbits over the highest skyscraper you got in your city," they answered him.

"If it's free and you don't sell anything nor take any money away from us while it is daylight and you are giving your performance, then here is your license permit," said the mayor speaking in the manner of a politician who has studied politics.

Thousands of people came to see the show on the public square. They wished to know how it would look to see five long-legged, spider jack-rabbits jump over the highest skyscraper in the city.

Four of the jack-rabbits had stripes. The fifth had stripes—and spots. Before they started the show Young Leather and Red Slippers held the jack-rabbits one by one in their arms and petted them, rubbed the feet and rubbed the long ears and ran their fingers along the long legs of the jumpers.

"Zingo," they yelled to the first jack-rabbit.

147

He got all ready. "And now zingo!" they yelled again. And the jack-rabbit took a run, lifted off his feet and went on and on and up and up till he went over the roof of the sky-scraper and then went down and down till he lit on his feet and came running on his long legs back to the public square where he started from, back where Young Leather and Red Slippers petted him and rubbed his long ears and said, "That's the boy."

Then three jack-rabbits made the jump over the skyscraper. "Zingo," they heard and got ready. "And now zingo," they heard and all three together in a row, their long ears touch-ing each other, they lifted off their feet and went on and on and up and up till they cleared the roof of the skyscraper. Then they came down and down till they lit on their feet and came running to the hands of Young Leather and Red Slippers to have their long legs and their long ears rubbed and petted.

Then came the turn of the fifth jack-rabbit,

the beautiful one with stripes and spots. "Ah, we're sorry to see you go, Ah-h, we're sorry," they said, rubbing his long ears and feeling of his long legs.

Then Young Leather and Red Slippers kissed him on the nose, kissed the last and fifth of the five long-legged spider jack-rabbits.

"Good-by, old bunny, good-by, you're the dandiest bunny there ever was," they whispered in his long ears. And he, because he knew what they were saying and why they were saying it, he wiggled his long ears and looked long and steady at them from his deep eyes.

"Zango," they yelled. He got ready. "And now zango!" they yelled again. And the fifth jack-rabbit with his stripes and spots lifted off his feet and went on and on and on and up and up and when he came to the roof of the skyscraper he kept on going on and on and up and up till after a while he was gone all the way out of sight.

They waited and watched, they watched

and waited. He never came back. He never was heard of again. He was gone. With the stripes on his back and the spots on his hair, he was gone. And Young Leather and Red Slippers said they were glad they had kissed him on the nose before he went away on a long trip far off, so far off he never came back.

The Wooden Indian and the Shaghorn Buffalo

One night a milk white moon was shining down on Main Street. The sidewalks and the stones, the walls and the windows all stood out milk white. And there was a thin blue mist drifted and shifted like a woman's veil up and down Main Street, up to the moon and back again. Yes, all Main Street was a mist blue and a milk white, mixed up and soft all over and all through.

It was past midnight. The Wooden Indian in front of the cigar store stepped down off his stand. The Shaghorn Buffalo in front of the haberdasher shop lifted his head and shook his whiskers, raised his hoofs out of his hoof-tracks.

Then—this is what happened. They moved straight toward each other. In the middle of Main Street they met. The Wooden Indian jumped straddle of the Shaghorn Buffalo. And the Shaghorn Buffalo put his head down and ran like a prairie wind straight west on Main Street.

At the high hill over the big bend of the Clear Green River they stopped. They stood looking. Drifting and shifting like a woman's blue veil, the blue mist filled the valley and the milk white moon filled the valley. And the mist and the moon touched with a lingering, wistful kiss the clear green water of the Clear Green River.

So they stood looking, the Wooden Indian with his copper face and wooden feathers, and the Shaghorn Buffalo with his big head and

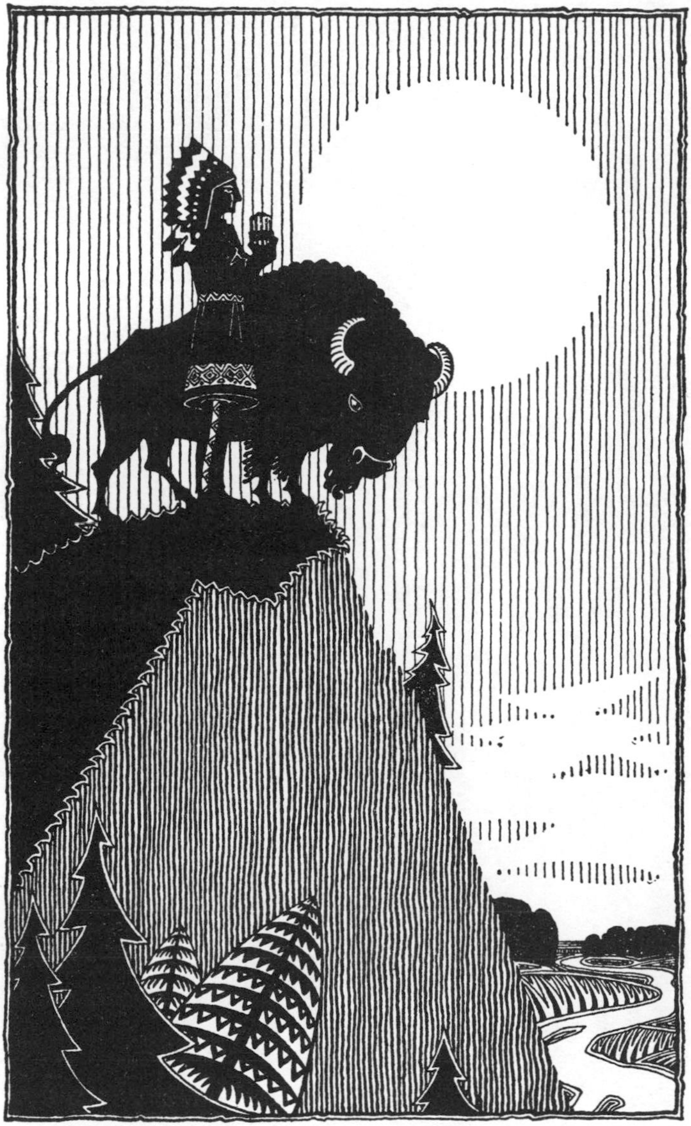

So they stood looking

heavy shoulders slumping down close to the ground.

And after they had looked a long while, and each of them got an eyeful of the high hill, the big bend and the moon mist on the river all blue and white and soft, after they had looked a long while, they turned around and the Shaghorn Buffalo put his head down and ran like a prairie wind down Main Street till he was exactly in front of the cigar store and the haberdasher shop. Then whisk! both of them were right back like they were before, standing still, taking whatever comes.

This is the story as it came from the night policeman of the Village of Cream Puffs. He told the people the next day, "I was sitting on the steps of the cigar store last night watching for burglars. And when I saw the Wooden Indian step down and the Shaghorn Buffalo step out, and the two of them go down Main Street like the wind, I says to myself, marvelish, 'tis marvelish, 'tis marvelish."

6. Four Stories About Dear, Dear Eyes

People: The White Horse Girl
The Blue Wind Boy
The Gray Man on Horseback
Six Girls With Balloons

Henry Hagglyhoagly
Susan Slackentwist
Two Wool Yarn Mittens

Peter Potato Blossom Wishes
Her Father
Many Shoes
Slippers
A Slipper Moon

The White Horse Girl and the Blue Wind Boy

When the dishes are washed at night time and the cool of the evening has come in summer or the lamps and fires are lit for the night in winter, then the fathers and mothers in the Rootabaga Country sometimes tell the young people the story of the White Horse Girl and the Blue Wind Boy.

The White Horse Girl grew up far in the west of the Rootabaga Country. All the years she grew up as a girl she liked to ride horses. Best of all things for her was to be straddle of a white horse loping with a loose bridle among the hills and along the rivers of the west Rootabaga Country.

She rode one horse white as snow, another horse white as new washed sheep wool, and another white as silver. And she could not tell because she did not know which of these three white horses she liked best.

"Snow is beautiful enough for me any time," she said, "new washed sheep wool, or silver out of a ribbon of the new moon, any or either is white enough for me. I like the white manes, the white flanks, the white noses, the white feet of all my ponies. I like the forelocks hanging down between the white ears of all three—my ponies."

And living neighbor to the White Horse Girl in the same prairie country, with the same black crows flying over their places, was the Blue Wind Boy. All the years he grew up as a boy he liked to walk with his feet in the dirt and the grass listening to the winds. Best of all things for him was to put on strong shoes and go hiking among the hills and along the rivers of the west Rootabaga Country, listening to the winds.

There was a blue wind of day time, starting sometimes six o'clock on a summer morning or eight o'clock on a winter morning. And there was a night wind with blue of summer stars in summer and blue of winter stars in winter. And there was yet another, a blue wind of the times between night and day, a blue dawn and evening wind. All three of these winds he liked so well he could not say which he liked best.

"The early morning wind is strong as the prairie and whatever I tell it I know it believes and remembers," he said, "and the night wind with the big dark curves of the night sky in it, the night wind gets inside of me and understands all my secrets. And the blue wind of the times between, in the dusk when it is neither night nor day, this is the wind that asks me questions and tells me to wait and it will bring me whatever I want."

Of course, it happened as it had to happen, the White Horse Girl and the Blue Wind Boy met. She, straddling one of her white horses, and he, wearing his strong hiking shoes in the dirt and the grass, it had to happen they should meet among the hills and along the rivers of the west Rootabaga Country where they lived neighbors.

And of course, she told him all about the snow white horse and the horse white as new washed sheep wool and the horse white as a silver ribbon of the new moon. And he told her all about the blue winds he liked listening to, the early morning wind, the night sky wind, and the wind of the dusk between, the wind that asked him questions and told him to wait.

One day the two of them were gone. On the same day of the week the White Horse Girl and the Blue Wind Boy went away. And their fathers and mothers and sisters and brothers and uncles and aunts wondered about them and talked about them, because they didn't tell anybody beforehand they were going. Nobody at all knew beforehand or afterward why they were going away, the real honest why of it.

They left a short letter. It read:

To All Our Sweethearts, Old Folks and Young Folks:
We have started to go where the white horses come from and where the blue winds begin. Keep a corner in your hearts for us while we are gone.
The White Horse Girl.
The Blue Wind Boy.

That was all they had to guess by in the west Rootabaga Country, to guess and guess where two darlings had gone.

Many years passed. One day there came riding across the Rootabaga Country a Gray Man on Horseback. He looked like he had come a long ways. So they asked him the question they always asked of any rider who looked like he had come a long ways, "Did you ever see the

White Horse Girl and the Blue Wind Boy?"

"Yes," he answered, "I saw them.

"It was a long, long ways from here I saw them," he went on, "it would take years and years to ride to where they are. They were sitting together and talking to each other, sometimes singing, in a place where the land runs high and tough rocks reach up. And they were looking out across water, blue water as far as the eye could see. And away far off the blue waters met the blue sky.

" 'Look!' said the Boy, 'that's where the blue winds begin.'

"And far out on the blue waters, just a little this side of where the blue winds begin, there were white manes, white flanks, white noses, white galloping feet.

" 'Look!' said the Girl, 'that's where the white horses come from.'

"And then nearer to the land came thousands in an hour, millions in a day, white horses, some white as snow, some like new washed sheep wool, some white as silver ribbons of the new moon.

"I asked them, 'Whose place is this?' They answered, 'It belongs to us; this is what we started for; this is where the white horses come from; this is where the blue winds begin.'"

And that was all the Gray Man on Horseback would tell the people of the west Rootabaga Country. That was all he knew, he said, and if there was any more he would tell it.

And the fathers and mothers and sisters and brothers and uncles and aunts of the White Horse Girl and the Blue Wind Boy wondered and talked often about whether the Gray Man on Horseback made up the story out of his head or whether it happened just like he told it.

Anyhow this is the story they tell sometimes to the young people of the west Rootabaga Country when the dishes are washed at night and the cool of the evening has come in summer or the lamps and fires are lit for the night in winter.

What Six Girls with Balloons Told the Gray Man on Horseback

Once there came riding across the Rootabaga Country a Gray Man on Horseback. He looked as if he had come a long ways. He looked like a brother to the same Gray Man on Horseback who said he had seen the White Horse Girl and the Blue Wind Boy.

He stopped in the Village of Cream Puffs. His gray face was sad and his eyes were gray deep and sad. He spoke short and seemed strong. Sometimes his eyes looked as if they were going to flash, but instead of fire they filled with shadows.

167

Yet—he did laugh once. It did happen once he lifted his head and face to the sky and let loose a long ripple of laughs.

On Main Street near the Roundhouse of the Big Spool, where they wind up the string that pulls the light little town back when the wind blows it away, there he was riding slow on his gray horse when he met six girls with six fine braids of yellow hair and six balloons apiece. That is, each and every one of the six girls had six fine long braids of yellow hair and each braid of hair had a balloon tied on the end. A little blue wind was blowing and the many balloons tied to the braids of the six girls swung up and down and slow and fast whenever the blue wind went up and down and slow and fast.

For the first time since he had been in the Village, the eyes of the Gray Man filled with lights and his face began to look hopeful. He stopped his horse when he came even with the six girls and the balloons floating from the braids of yellow hair.

168

"Where you going?" he asked.

"Who—hoo-hoo? Who—who—who?" the six girls cheeped out.

"All six of you and your balloons, where you going?"

"Oh, hoo-hoo-hoo, back where we came from," and they all turned their heads back and forth and sideways, which of course turned all the balloons back and forth and sideways because the balloons were fastened to the fine braids of hair which were fastened to their heads.

"And where do you go when you get back where you came from?" he asked just to be asking.

"Oh, hoo-hoo-hoo, then we start out and go straight ahead and see what we can see," they all answered just to be answering and they dipped their heads and swung them up which of course dipped all the balloons and swung them up.

So they talked, he asking just to be asking

169

and the six balloon girls answering just to be answering.

At last his sad mouth broke into a smile and his eyes were lit like a morning sun coming up over harvest fields. And he said to them, "Tell me why are balloons—that is what I want you to tell me—why are balloons?"

The first little girl put her thumb under her chin, looked up at her six balloons floating in the little blue wind over her head, and said: "Balloons are wishes. The wind made them. The west wind makes the red balloons. The south wind makes the blue. The yellow and green balloons come from the east wind and the north wind."

The second little girl put her first finger next to her nose, looked up at her six balloons dipping up and down like hill flowers in a small wind, and said:

"A balloon used to be a flower. It got tired. Then it changed itself to a balloon. I listened one time to a yellow balloon. It was talking

170

to itself like people talk. It said, 'I used to be a yellow pumpkin flower stuck down close to the ground, now I am a yellow balloon high up in the air where nobody can walk on me and I can see everything.' "

The third little girl held both of her ears like she was afraid they would wiggle while she slid with a skip, turned quick, and looking up at her balloons, spoke these words:

"A balloon is foam. It comes the same as soap bubbles come. A long time ago it used to be sliding along on water, river water, ocean water, waterfall water, falling and falling over a rocky waterfall, any water you want. The wind saw the bubble and picked it up and carried it away, telling it, 'Now you're a balloon—come along and see the world.' "

The fourth little girl jumped straight into the air so all six of her balloons made a jump like they were going to get loose and go to the sky—and when the little girl came down from her jump and was standing on her two feet with her head turned looking up at the six balloons, she spoke the shortest answer of all, saying:

"Balloons are to make us look up. They help our necks."

The fifth little girl stood first on one foot, then another, bent her head down to her knees and looked at her toes, then swinging straight up and looking at the flying spotted yellow and red and green balloons, she said:

"Balloons come from orchards. Look for trees where half is oranges and half is orange balloons. Look for apple trees where half is red pippins and half is red pippin balloons. Look for watermelons too. A long green balloon with white and yellow belly stripes is a ghost. It came from a watermelon said goodby."

The sixth girl, the last one, kicked the heel of her left foot with the toe of her right foot, put her thumbs under her ears and wiggled all her fingers, then stopped all her kicking and wiggling, and stood looking up at her balloons all quiet because the wind had gone down—and she murmured like she was thinking to herself:

"Balloons come from fire chasers. Every balloon has a fire chaser chasing it. All the fire chasers are made terrible quick and when they come they burn quick, so the balloon is made light so it can run away terrible quick. Balloons slip away from fire. If they don't they can't be balloons. Running away from fire keeps them light."

All the time he listened to the six girls the face of the Gray Man kept getting more hopeful. His eyes lit up. Twice he smiled. And after he said good-by and rode up the street, he lifted his head and face to the sky and let loose a long ripple of laughs.

He kept looking back when he left the Village and the last thing he saw was the six girls each with six balloons fastened to the six braids of yellow hair hanging down their backs.

The sixth little girl kicked the heel of her

left foot with the toe of her right foot and said, "He is a nice man. I think he must be our uncle. If he comes again we shall all ask him to tell us where he thinks balloons come from."

And the other five girls all answered, "Yes," or "Yes, yes," or "Yes, yes, yes," real fast like a balloon with a fire chaser after it.

How Henry Hagglyhoagly Played the Guitar with His Mittens On

Sometimes in January the sky comes down close if we walk on a country road, and turn our faces up to look at the sky.

Sometimes on that kind of a January night the stars look like numbers, look like the arithmetic writing of a girl going to school and just beginning arithmetic.

It was this kind of a night Henry Hagglyhoagly was walking down a country road on his way to the home of Susan Slackentwist, the daughter of the rutabaga king near the Village of Liver-and-Onions. When Henry Hagglyhoagly turned his face up to look at the sky it seemed to him as though the sky came down close to his nose, and there was a writing in stars as though some girl had been doing arithmetic examples, writing number 4 and number 7 and 4 and 7 over and over again across the sky.

"Why is it so bitter cold weather?" Henry Hagglyhoagly asked himself, "if I say many bitter bitters it is not so bitter as the cold wind and the cold weather."

"You are good, mittens, keeping my fingers warm," he said every once in a while to the wool yarn mittens on his hands.

The wind came tearing along and put its chilly, icy, clammy clamps on the nose of Henry Hagglyhoagly, fastening the clamps like a nipping, gripping clothes pin on his nose. He put his wool yarn mittens up on his nose and rubbed till the wind took off the chilly, icy, clammy

It seemed to him as though the sky came down close
to his nose

clamps. His nose was warm again; he said, "Thank you, mittens, for keeping my nose warm."

He spoke to his wool yarn mittens as though they were two kittens or pups, or two little cub bears, or two little Idaho ponies. "You're my chums keeping me company," he said to the mittens.

"Do you know what we got here under our left elbow?" he said to the mittens, "I shall mention to you what is here under my left elbow.

"It ain't a mandolin, it ain't a mouth organ nor an accordion nor a concertina nor a fiddle. It is a guitar, a Spanish Spinnish Splishy guitar made special.

"Yes, mittens, they said a strong young man like me ought to have a piano because a piano is handy to play for everybody in the house and a piano is handy to put a hat and overcoat on or books or flowers.

"I snizzled at 'em, mittens. I told 'em I

seen a Spanish Spinnish Splishy guitar made special in a hardware store window for eight dollars and a half.

"And so, mittens—are you listening, mittens?—after cornhusking was all husked and the oats thrashing all thrashed and the rutabaga digging all dug, I took eight dollars and a half in my inside vest pocket and I went to the hardware store.

"I put my thumbs in my vest pocket and I wiggled my fingers like a man when he is proud of what he is going to have if he gets it. And I said to the head clerk in the hardware store, 'Sir, the article I desire to purchase this evening as one of your high class customers, the article I desire to have after I buy it for myself, is the article there in the window, sir, the Spanish Spinnish Splishy guitar.'

"And, mittens, if you are listening, I am taking this Spanish Spinnish Splishy guitar to go to the home of Susan Slackentwist, the daughter of the rutabaga king near the Village of

Liver-and-Onions, to sing a serenade song."

The cold wind of the bitter cold weather blew and blew, trying to blow the guitar out from under the left elbow of Henry Haggly-hoagly. And the worse the wind blew the tighter he held his elbow holding the guitar where he wanted it.

He walked on and on with his long legs stepping long steps till at last he stopped, held his nose in the air, and sniffed.

"Do I sniff something or do I not?" he asked, lifting his wool yarn mittens to his nose and rubbing his nose till it was warm. Again he sniffed.

"Ah hah, yeah, yeah, this is the big rutabaga field near the home of the rutabaga king and the home of his daughter, Susan Slackentwist."

At last he came to the house, stood under the window and slung the guitar around in front of him to play the music to go with the song.

"And now," he asked his mittens, "shall I take you off or keep you on? If I take you off the cold wind of the bitter cold weather will freeze my hands so stiff and bitter cold my fingers will be too stiff to play the guitar. *I will play with mittens on.*"

Which he did. He stood under the window of Susan Slackentwist and played the guitar with his mittens on, the warm wool yarn mittens he called his chums. It was the first time any strong young man going to see his sweetheart ever played the guitar with his mittens on when it was a bitter night with a cold wind and cold weather.

Susan Slackentwist opened her window and threw him a snow-bird feather to keep for a keepsake to remember her by. And for years afterward many a sweetheart in the Rootabaga Country told her lover, "If you wish to marry me let me hear you under my window on a winter night playing the guitar with wool yarn mittens on."

And when Henry Hagglyhoagly walked home on his long legs stepping long steps, he

The Guitar with His Mittens On

said to his mittens, "This Spanish Spinnish Splishy guitar made special will bring us luck." And when he turned his face up, the sky came down close and he could see stars fixed like numbers and the arithmetic writing of a girl going to school learning to write number 4 and number 7 and 4 and 7 over and over.

Never Kick a Slipper at the Moon

When a girl is growing up in the Rootabaga Country she learns some things to do, some things *not* to do.

"Never kick a slipper at the moon if it is the time for the Dancing Slipper Moon when the slim early moon looks like the toe and the heel of a dancer's foot," was the advice Mr. Wishes, the father of Peter Potato Blossom Wishes, gave to his daughter.

"Why?" she asked him.

"Because your slipper will go straight up, on and on to the moon, and fasten itself on the moon as if the moon is a foot ready for dancing," said Mr. Wishes.

Never Kick a Slipper at the Moon

"A long time ago there was one night when a secret word was passed around to all the shoes standing in the bedrooms and closets.

"The whisper of the secret was: 'To-night all the shoes and the slippers and the boots of the world are going walking without any feet in them. To-night when those who put us on their feet in the daytime, are sleeping in their beds, we all get up and walk and go walking where we walk in the daytime.'

"And in the middle of the night, when the people in the beds were sleeping, the shoes and the slippers and the boots everywhere walked out of the bedrooms and the closets. Along the sidewalks on the streets, up and down stairways, along hallways, the shoes and slippers and the boots tramped and marched and stumbled.

"Scme walked pussyfoot, sliding easy and soft just like people in the daytime. Some walked clumping and clumping, coming down heavy on the heels and slow on the toes, just like people in the daytime.

Never Kick a Slipper at the Moon

"Some turned their toes in and walked pigeon-toe, some spread their toes out and held their heels in, just like people in the daytime. Some ran glad and fast, some lagged slow and sorry.

"Now there was a little girl in the Village of Cream Puffs who came home from a dance that night. And she was tired from dancing round dances and square dances, one steps and two steps, toe dances and toe and heel dances, dances close up and dances far apart, she was so tired she took off only one slipper, tumbled onto her bed and went to sleep with one slipper on.

"She woke up in the morning when it was yet dark. And she went to the window and looked up in the sky and saw a Dancing Slipper Moon dancing far and high in the deep blue sea of the moon sky.

" 'Oh—what a moon—what a dancing slipper of a moon!' she cried with a little song to herself.

Never Kick a Slipper at the Moon

"She opened the window, saying again, 'Oh! what a moon!'—and kicked her foot with the slipper on it straight toward the moon.

"The slipper flew off and flew up and went on and on and up and up in the moonshine.

"It never came back, that slipper. It was never seen again. When they asked the girl about it she said, 'It slipped off my foot and went up and up and the last I saw of it the slipper was going on straight to the moon.'"

And these are the explanations why fathers and mothers in the Rootabaga Country say to their girls growing up, "Never kick a slipper at the moon if it is the time of the Dancing Slipper Moon when the ends of the moon look like the toe and the heel of a dancer's foot."

7. One Story — "Only the Fire-Born Understand Blue"

> *People:* Fire the Goat
> Flim the Goose
> Shadows

Sand Flat Shadows

Fire the Goat and Flim the Goose slept out.
Stub pines stood over them. And away up next
over the stub pines were stars.

It was a white sand flat they slept on. The
floor of the sand flat ran straight to the Big
Lake of the Booming Rollers.

And just over the sand flat and just over the
booming rollers was a high room where the
mist people were making pictures. Gray pictures, blue and sometimes a little gold, and often
silver, were the pictures.

And next just over the high room where the
mist people were making pictures, next just
over were the stars.

Over everything and always last and highest of all, were the stars.

Fire the Goat took off his horns. Flim the Goose took off his wings. "This is where we sleep," they said to each other, "here in the stub pines on the sand flats next to the booming rollers and high over everything and always last and highest of all, the stars."

Fire the Goat laid his horns under his head. Flim the Goose laid his wings under his head. "This is the best place for what you want to keep," they said to each other. Then they crossed their fingers for luck and lay down and went to sleep and slept. And while they slept the mist people went on making pictures. Gray pictures, blue and sometimes a little gold but more often silver, such were the pictures the mist people went on making while Fire the Goat and Flim the Goose went on sleeping. And over everything and always last and highest of all, were the stars.

They woke up. Fire the Goat took his horns

out and put them on. "It's morning now," he said.

Flim the Goose took his wings out and put them on. "It's another day now," he said.

Then they sat looking. Away off where the sun was coming up, inching and pushing up far across the rim curve of the Big Lake of the Booming Rollers, along the whole line of the east sky, there were people and animals, all black or all so gray they were near black.

There was a big horse with his mouth open, ears laid back, front legs thrown in two curves like harvest sickles.

There was a camel with two humps, moving slow and grand like he had all the time of all the years of all the world to go in.

There was an elephant without any head, with six short legs. There were many cows. There was a man with a club over his shoulder and a woman with a bundle on the back of her neck.

And they marched on. They were going

nowhere, it seemed. And they were going slow. They had plenty of time. There was nothing else to do. It was fixed for them to do it, long ago it was fixed. And so they were marching.

Sometimes the big horse's head sagged and dropped off and came back again. Sometimes the humps of the camel sagged and dropped off and came back again. And sometimes the club on the man's shoulder got bigger and heavier and the man staggered under it and then his legs got bigger and stronger and he steadied himself and went on. And again sometimes the bundle on the back of the neck of the woman got bigger and heavier and the bundle sagged and the woman staggered and her legs got bigger and stronger and she steadied herself and went on.

This was the show, the hippodrome, the spectacular circus that passed on the east sky before the eyes of Fire the Goat and Flim the Goose.

"Which is this, who are they and why do

Away off where the sun was coming up, there were
people and animals

they come?" Flim the Goose asked Fire the Goat.

"Do you ask me because you wish me to tell you?" asked Fire the Goat.

"Indeed it is a question to which I want an honest answer."

"Has never the father or mother nor the uncle or aunt nor the kith and kin of Flim the Goose told him the what and the which of this?"

"Never has the such of this which been put here this way to me by anybody."

Flim the Goose held up his fingers and said, "I don't talk to you with my fingers crossed."

And so Fire the Goat began to explain to Flim the Goose all about the show, the hippodrome, the mastodonic cyclopean spectacle which was passing on the east sky in front of the sun coming up.

"People say they are shadows," began Fire the Goat. "That is a name, a word, a little cough and a couple of syllables.

"For some people shadows are comic and only to laugh at. For some other people shadows are like a mouth and its breath. The breath comes out and it is nothing. It is like air and nobody can make it into a package and carry it away. It will not melt like gold nor can you shovel it like cinders. So to these people it means nothing.

"And then there are other people," Fire the Goat went on. "There are other people who understand shadows. The fire-born understand. The fire-born know where shadows come from and why they are.

"Long ago, when the Makers of the World were done making the round earth, the time came when they were ready to make the animals to put on the earth. They were not sure how to make the animals. They did not know what shape animals they wanted.

"And so they practised. They did not make real animals at first. They made only shapes of animals. And these shapes were shadows,

198

shadows like these you and I, Fire the Goat and Flim the Goose, are looking at this morning across the booming rollers on the east sky where the sun is coming up.

"The shadow horse over there on the east sky with his mouth open, his ears laid back, and his front legs thrown in a curve like harvest sickles, that shadow horse was one they made long ago when they were practising to make a real horse. That shadow horse was a mistake and they threw him away. Never will you see two shadow horses alike. All shadow horses on the sky are different. Each one is a mistake, a shadow horse thrown away because he was not good enough to be a real horse.

"That elephant with no head on his neck, stumbling so grand on six legs—and that grand camel with two humps, one bigger than the other—and those cows with horns in front and behind—they are all mistakes, they were all thrown away because they were not made good enough to be real elephants, real cows, real carr.els. They were made just for practice, away back early in the world before any real animals came on their legs to eat and live and be here like the rest of us.

"That man—see him now staggering along with the club over his shoulder—see how his long arms come to his knees and sometimes his hands drag below his feet. See how heavy the club on his shoulders loads him down and drags him on. He is one of the oldest shadow men. He was a mistake and they threw him away. He was made just for practice.

"And that woman. See her now at the end of that procession across the booming rollers on the east sky. See her the last of all, the end of the procession. On the back of her neck a bundle. Sometimes the bundle gets bigger. The woman staggers. Her legs get bigger and stronger. She picks herself up and goes along shaking her head. She is the same as the others. She is a shadow and she was made as a mistake.

Sand Flat Shadows

Early, early in the beginnings of the world she was made, for practice.

"Listen, Flim the Goose. What I am telling you is a secret of the fire-born. I do not know whether you understand. We have slept together a night on the sand flats next to the booming rollers, under the stub pines with the stars high over—and so I tell what the fathers of the fire-born tell their sons."

And that day Fire the Goat and Flim the Goose moved along the sand flat shore of the Big Lake of the Booming Rollers. It was a blue day, with a fire-blue of the sun mixing itself in the air and the water. Off to the north the booming rollers were blue sea-green. To the east they were sometimes streak purple, sometimes changing bluebell stripes. And to the south they were silver blue, sheet blue.

Where the shadow hippodrome marched on the east sky that morning was a long line of blue-bird spots.

"Only the fire-born understand blue," said Fire the Goat to Flim the Goose. And that night as the night before they slept on a sand flat. And again Fire the Goat took off his horns and laid them under his head while he slept and Flim the Goose took off his wings and laid them under his head while he slept.

And twice in the night, Fire the Goat whispered in his sleep, whispered to the stars, "Only the fire-born understand blue."

8. Two Stories About Corn Fairies, Blue Foxes, Flongboos and Happenings That Happened in the United States and Canada

People: Spink
Skabootch
A Man
Corn Fairies

Blue Foxes
Flongboos
A Philadelphia Policeman
Passenger Conductor
Chicago Newspapers
The Head Spotter of the Weather Makers at Medicine Hat

How to Tell Corn Fairies If You See 'Em

If you have ever watched the little corn begin to march across the black lands and then slowly change to big corn and go marching on from the little corn moon of summer to the big corn harvest moon of autumn, then you must have guessed who it is that helps the corn come along. It is the corn fairies. Leave out the corn fairies and there wouldn't be any corn.

All children know this. All boys and girls know that corn is no good unless there are corn fairies.

Have you ever stood in Illinois or Iowa and

watched the late summer wind or the early fall wind running across a big cornfield? It looks as if a big, long blanket were being spread out for dancers to come and dance on. If you look close and if you listen close you can see the corn fairies come dancing and singing—sometimes. If it is a wild day and a hot sun is pouring down while a cool north wind blows—and this happens sometimes—then you will be sure to see thousands of corn fairies marching and countermarching in mocking grand marches over the big, long blanket of green and silver. Then too they sing, only you must listen with your littlest and newest ears if you wish to hear their singing. They sing soft songs that go pla-sizzy pla-sizzy-sizzy, and each song is softer than an eye wink, softer than a Nebraska baby's thumb.

And Spink, who is a little girl living in the same house with the man writing this story, and Skabootch, who is another little girl in the same house—both Spink and Skabootch are asking the question, "How can we tell corn fairies if we see 'em? If we meet a corn fairy how will we know it?" And this is the explanation the man gave to Spink who is older than Skabootch, and to Skabootch who is younger than Spink:—

All corn fairies wear overalls. They work hard, the corn fairies, and they are proud. The reason they are proud is because they work so hard. And the reason they work so hard is because they have overalls.

But understand this. The overalls are corn gold cloth, woven from leaves of ripe corn mixed with ripe October corn silk. In the first week of the harvest moon coming up red and changing to yellow and silver the corn fairies sit by thousands between the corn rows weaving and stitching the clothes they have to wear next winter, next spring, next summer.

They sit cross-legged when they sew. And it is a law among them each one must point the big toe at the moon while sewing the harvest moon clothes. When the moon comes up red as blood early in the evening they point their big toes slanting toward the east. Then towards midnight when the moon is yellow and half way up the sky their big toes are only half slanted as they sit cross-legged sewing. And after midnight when the moon sails its silver disk high overhead and toward the west, then the corn fairies sit sewing with their big toes pointed nearly straight up.

If it is a cool night and looks like frost, then the laughter of the corn fairies is something worth seeing. All the time they sit sewing their next year clothes they are laughing. It is not a law they have to laugh. They laugh because they are half-tickled and glad because it is a good corn year.

And whenever the corn fairies laugh then the laugh comes out of the mouth like a thin gold frost. If you should be lucky enough to see a thousand corn fairies sitting between the corn rows and all of them laughing, you would laugh with wonder yourself to see the gold frost coming from their mouths while they laughed.

If You See 'Em

Travelers who have traveled far, and seen many things, say that if you know the corn fairies with a real knowledge you can always tell by the stitches in their clothes what state they are from.

In Illinois the corn fairies stitch fifteen stitches of ripe corn silk across the woven corn leaf cloth. In Iowa they stitch sixteen stitches, in Nebraska seventeen, and the farther west you go the more corn silk stitches the corn fairies have in the corn cloth clothes they wear.

In Minnesota one year there were fairies with a blue sash of corn-flowers across the breast. In the Dakotas the same year all the fairies wore pumpkin-flower neckties, yellow four-in-hands and yellow ascots. And in one strange year it happened in both the states of Ohio and Texas the corn fairies wore little wristlets of white morning glories.

The traveler who heard about this asked many questions and found out the reason why that year the corn fairies wore little wristlets of white morning glories. He said, "Whenever fairies are sad they wear white. And this year, which was long ago, was the year men were tearing down all the old zigzag rail fences. Now those old zigzag rail fences were beautiful for the fairies because a hundred fairies could sit on one rail and thousands and thousands of them could sit on the zigzags and sing pla-sizzy pla-sizzy, softer than an eye-wink, softer than a baby's thumb, all on a moonlight summer night. And they found out that year was going to be the last year of the zigzag rail fences. It made them sorry and sad, and when they are sorry and sad they wear white. So they picked the wonderful white morning glories running along the zigzag rail fences and made them into little wristlets and wore those wristlets the next year to show they were sorry and sad."

Of course, all this helps you to know how the corn fairies look in the evening, the night

time and the moonlight. Now we shall see
how they look in the day time.

In the day time the corn fairies have their
overalls of corn gold cloth on. And they walk
among the corn rows and climb the corn stalks
and fix things in the leaves and stalks and ears
of the corn. They help it to grow.

Each one carries on the left shoulder a mouse
brush to brush away the field mice. And over
the right shoulder each one has a cricket broom
to sweep away the crickets. The brush is a
whisk brush to brush away mice that get foolish.
And the broom is to sweep away crickets that
get foolish.

Around the middle of each corn fairy is a yellow-belly belt. And stuck in this belt is a purple moon shaft hammer. Whenever the wind
blows strong and nearly blows the corn down,
then the fairies run out and take their purple
moon shaft hammers out of their yellow-belly
belts and nail down nails to keep the corn from

blowing down. When a rain storm is blowing up terrible and driving all kinds of terribles across the cornfield, then you can be sure of one thing. Running like the wind among the corn rows are the fairies, jerking their purple moon shaft hammers out of their belts and nailing nails down to keep the corn standing up so it will grow and be ripe and beautiful when the harvest moon comes again in the fall.

Spink and Skabootch ask where the corn fairies get the nails. The answer to Spink and Skabootch is, "Next week you will learn all about where the corn fairies get the nails to nail down the corn if you will keep your faces washed and your ears washed till next week."

And the next time you stand watching a big cornfield in late summer or early fall, when the wind is running across the green and silver, listen with your littlest and newest ears. Maybe you will hear the corn fairies going pla-sizzy pla-sizzy-sizzy, softer than an eye wink, softer than a Nebraska baby's thumb.

How the Animals Lost Their Tails and Got Them Back Traveling From Philadelphia to Medicine Hat

Far up in North America, near the Saskatchewan river, in the Winnipeg wheat country, not so far from the town of Moose Jaw named for the jaw of a moose shot by a hunter there, up where the blizzards and the chinooks begin, where nobody works unless they have to and they nearly all have to, there stands the place known as Medicine Hat.

And there on a high stool in a high tower

on a high hill sits the Head Spotter of the Weather Makers.

When the animals lost their tails it was because the Head Spotter of the Weather Makers at Medicine Hat was careless.

The tails of the animals were stiff and dry because for a long while there was dusty dry weather. Then at last came rain. And the water from the sky poured on the tails of the animals and softened them.

Then the chilly chills came whistling with icy mittens and they froze all the tails stiff. A big wind blew up and blew and blew till all the tails of the animals blew off.

It was easy for the fat stub hogs with their fat stub tails. But it was not so easy for the blue fox who uses his tail to help him when he runs, when he eats, when he walks or talks, when he makes pictures or writes letters in the snow or when he puts a snack of bacon meat with stripes of fat and lean to hide till he wants it under a big rock by a river.

There on a high stool in a high tower, on a high hill
sits the Head Spotter of the Weather Makers

It was easy enough for the rabbit who has long ears and no tail at all except a white thumb of cotton. But it was hard for the yellow flongboo who at night lights up his house in a hollow tree with his fire yellow torch of a tail. It is hard for the yellow flongboo to lose his tail because it lights up his way when he sneaks at night on the prairie, sneaking up on the flangwayers, the hippers and hangjasts, so good to eat.

The animals picked a committee of representatives to represent them in a parleyhoo to see what steps could be taken by talking to do something. There were sixty-six representatives on the committee and they decided to call it the Committee of Sixty Six. It was a distinguished committee and when they all sat together holding their mouths under their noses (just like a distinguished committee) and blinking their eyes up over their noses and cleaning their ears and scratching themselves under the chin looking thoughtful (just like a distinguished committee) then anybody would say just to look at them, "This must be quite a distinguished committee."

Of course, they would all have looked more distinguished if they had had their tails on. If the big wavy streak of a blue tail blows off behind a blue fox, he doesn't look near so distinguished. Or, if the long yellow torch of a tail blows off behind a yellow flongboo, he doesn't look so distinguished as he did before the wind blew.

So the Committee of Sixty Six had a meeting and a parleyhoo to decide what steps could be taken by talking to do something. For chairman they picked an old flongboo who was an umpire and used to umpire many mix-ups. Among the flongboos he was called "the umpire of umpires," "the king of umpires," "the prince of umpires," "the peer of umpires." When there was a fight and a snag and a wrangle between two families living next door neighbors to each other and this old flongboo was called in to umpire and to say which family was right and which family was wrong, which family started it and which family ought to stop it, he used to say, "The best umpire is the one who knows just how far to go and how far not to go." He was from Massachusetts, born near Chappaquiddick, this old flongboo, and he lived there in a horse chestnut tree six feet thick half way between South Hadley and Northampton. And at night, before he lost his tail, he lighted up the big hollow cave inside the horse chestnut tree with his yellow torch of a tail.

After he was nominated with speeches and elected with votes to be the chairman, he stood up on the platform and took a gavel and banged with the gavel and made the Committee of Sixty Six come to order.

"It is no picnic to lose your tail and we are here for business," he said, banging his gavel again.

A blue fox from Waco, Texas, with his ears

full of dry bluebonnet leaves from a hole where he lived near the Brazos river, stood up and said, "Mr. Chairman, do I have the floor?"

"You have whatever you get away with—I get your number," said the chairman.

"I make a motion," said the blue fox from Waco, "and I move you, Sir, that this committee get on a train at Philadelphia and ride on the train till it stops and then take another train and take more trains and keep on riding till we get to Medicine Hat, near the Saskatchewan river, in the Winnipeg wheat country where the Head Spotter of the Weather Makers sits on a high stool in a high tower on a high hill spotting the weather. There we will ask him if he will respectfully let us beseech him to bring back weather that will bring back our tails. It was the weather took away our tails; it is the weather can bring back our tails."

"All in favor of the motion," said the chairman, "will clean their right ears with their right paws."

And all the blue foxes and all the yellow flongboos began cleaning their right ears with their right paws.

"All who are against the motion will clean their left ears with their left paws," said the chairman.

And all the blue foxes and all the yellow flongboos began cleaning their left ears with their left paws.

"The motion is carried both ways—it is a razmataz," said the chairman. "Once again, all in favor of the motion will stand up on the toes of their hind legs and stick their noses straight up in the air." And all the blue foxes and all the yellow flongboos stood up on the toes of their hind legs and stuck their noses straight up in the air.

"And now," said the chairman, "all who are against the motion will stand on the top and the apex of their heads, stick their hind legs straight up in the air, and make a noise like a woof woof."

And then not one of the blue foxes and not one of the yellow flongboos stood on the top and the apex of his head nor stuck his hind legs up in the air nor made a noise like a woof woof.

"The motion is carried and this is no picnic," said the chairman.

So the committee went to Philadelphia to get on a train to ride on.

"Would you be so kind as to tell us the way to the union depot," the chairman asked a policeman. It was the first time a flongboo ever spoke to a policeman on the streets of Philadelphia.

"It pays to be polite," said the policeman.

"May I ask you again if you would kindly direct us to the union depot? We wish to ride on a train," said the flongboo.

"Polite persons and angry persons are different kinds," said the policeman.

The flongboo's eyes changed their lights and a slow torch of fire sprang out behind where his tail used to be. And speaking to the policeman, he said, "Sir, I must inform you, publicly and respectfully, that we are The Committee of Sixty Six. We are honorable and distinguished representatives from places your honest and ignorant geography never told you about. This committee is going to ride on the cars to Medicine Hat near the Saskatchewan river in the Winnipeg wheat country where the blizzards and chinooks begin. We have a special message and a secret errand for the Head Spotter of the Weather Makers."

"I am a polite friend of all respectable people —that is why I wear this star to arrest people who are not respectable," said the policeman, touching with his pointing finger the silver and nickel star fastened with a safety pin on his blue uniform coat.

"This is the first time ever in the history of the United States that a committee of sixty-six blue foxes and flongboos has ever visited a city in the United States," insinuated the flongboo.

"I beg to be mistaken," finished the policeman. "The union depot is under that clock." And he pointed to a clock near by.

"I thank you for myself, I thank you for the Committee of Sixty Six, I thank you for the sake of all the animals in the United States who have lost their tails," finished the chairman.

Over to the Philadelphia union depot they went, all sixty-six, half blue foxes, half flongboos. As they pattered pitty-pat, pitty-pat, each with feet and toenails, ears and hair, everything but tails, into the Philadelphia union depot, they had nothing to say. And yet though they had nothing to say the passengers in the union depot waiting for trains thought they had something to say and were saying it. So the passengers in the union depot waiting for trains listened. But with all their listening the passengers never heard the blue foxes and yellow flongboos say anything.

"They are saying it to each other in some

224

strange language from where they belong," said one passenger waiting for a train.

"They have secrets to keep among each other, and never tell us," said another passenger.

"We will find out all about it reading the newspapers upside down to-morrow morning," said a third passenger.

Then the blue foxes and the yellow flongboos pattered pitty-pat, pitty-pat, each with feet and toenails, ears and hair, everything except tails, pattered scritch scratch over the stone floors out into the train shed. They climbed into a special smoking car hooked on ahead of the engine.

"This car hooked on ahead of the engine was put on special for us so we will always be ahead and we will get there before the train does," said the chairman to the committee.

The train ran out of the train shed. It kept on the tracks and never left the rails. It came to the Horseshoe Curve near Altoona where the tracks bend like a big horseshoe. Instead of going around the long winding bend of the horseshoe tracks up and around the mountains, the train acted different. The train jumped off the tracks down into the valley and cut across in a straight line on a cut-off, jumped on the tracks again and went on toward Ohio.

The conductor said, "If you are going to jump the train off the tracks, tell us about it beforehand."

"When we lost our tails nobody told us about it beforehand," said the old flongboo umpire.

Two baby blue foxes, the youngest on the committee, sat on the front platform. Mile after mile of chimneys went by. Four hundred smokestacks stood in a row and tubs on tubs of sooty black soot marched out.

"This is the place where the black cats come to be washed," said the first baby blue fox.

"I believe your affidavit," said the second blue fox.

Crossing Ohio and Indiana at night the flongboos took off the roof of the car. The conductor told them, "I must have an explanation." "It was between us and the stars," they told him.

The train ran into Chicago. That afternoon there were pictures upside down in the newspapers showing the blue foxes and the yellow flongboos climbing telephone poles standing on their heads eating pink ice cream with iron axes.

Each blue fox and yellow flongboo got a newspaper for himself and each one looked long and careful upside down to see how he looked in the picture in the newspaper climbing a telephone pole standing on his head eating pink ice cream with an iron ax.

Crossing Minnesota the sky began to fill with the snow ghosts of Minnesota snow weather. Again the foxes and flongboos lifted the roof off the car, telling the conductor they would rather wreck the train than miss the big show of the snow ghosts of the first Minnesota snow weather of the winter.

Some went to sleep but the two baby blue foxes stayed up all night watching the snow ghosts and telling snow ghost stories to each other.

Early in the night the first baby blue fox said to the second, "Who are the snow ghosts the ghosts of?" The second baby blue fox answered, "Everybody who makes a snowball, a snow man, a snow fox or a snow fish or a snow pattycake, everybody has a snow ghost."

And that was only the beginning of their talk. It would take a big book to tell all that the two baby foxes told each other that night about the Minnesota snow ghosts, because they sat up all night telling old stories their fathers and mothers and grandfathers and grandmothers told them, and making up new stories never heard before about where the snow ghosts go on Christmas morning and how the snow ghosts watch the New Year in.

Tails and Got Them Back

Somewhere between Winnipeg and Moose Jaw, somewhere it was they stopped the train and all ran out in the snow where the white moon was shining down a valley of birch trees. It was the Snowbird Valley where all the snowbirds of Canada come early in the winter and make their snow shoes.

At last they came to Medicine Hat, near the Saskatchewan River, where the blizzards and the chinooks begin, where nobody works unless they have to and they nearly all have to. There they ran in the snow till they came to the place where the Head Spotter of the Weather Makers sits on a high stool in a high tower on a high hill watching the weather.

"Let loose another big wind to blow back our tails to us, let loose a big freeze to freeze our tails onto us again, and so let us get back our lost tails," they said to the Head Spotter of the Weather Makers.

Which was just what he did, giving them exactly what they wanted, so they all went back

home satisfied, the blue foxes each with a big
wavy brush of a tail to help him when he runs,
when he eats, when he walks or talks, when
he makes pictures or writes letters in the snow
or when he puts a snack of bacon meat with
stripes of fat and lean to hide till he wants it
under a big rock by the river—and the yellow
flongboos each with a long yellow torch of a
tail to light up his home in a hollow tree or to
light up his way when he sneaks at night on
the prairie, sneaking up on the flangwayer, the
hipper or the hangjast.

A Selected List of Voyager Books

AVB 40 Jeanette Eaton
LONE JOURNEY

AVB 41 Anne Guthrie
MADAME AMBASSADOR

AVB 42 Leif Hamre
LEAP INTO DANGER

AVB 43 Carol Kendall
THE GAMMAGE CUP

AVB 44 Stephen W. Meader
WHO RIDES IN THE DARK?

AVB 45 Joan Phipson
THE FAMILY CONSPIRACY

AVB 46 Kathrene Pinkerton
HIDDEN HARBOR

AVB 47 Sigurd Senje
ESCAPE!

AVB 48 Miriam Young
THE SECRET OF STONE HOUSE FARM

AVB 49 Karin Anckarsvärd
THE ROBBER GHOST

AVB 50 Eleanor Estes
THE MOFFATS

AVB 51 Carolyn Haywood
"B" IS FOR BETSY

AVB 52 Eleanor F. Lattimore
LITTLE PEAR

AVB 53 Dorothy Lyons
BLUE SMOKE

AVB 54 Stephen W. Meader
SPARKPLUG OF THE HORNETS

AVB 55 Andre Norton
STAND TO HORSE

AVB 56 William O. Steele
THE BUFFALO KNIFE

AVB 57 Karin Anckarsvärd
MADCAP MYSTERY

AVB 58 Harold Courlander
THE KING'S DRUM

AVB 59 Edward Eager
HALF MAGIC

AVB 60 Mary Norton
THE BORROWERS AFIELD

AVB 61 E. C. Spykman
EDIE ON THE WARPATH

AVB 65 Eleanor Estes
GINGER PYE

AVB 69 Virginia Sorensen
MIRACLES ON MAPLE HILL

AVB 70 William O. Steele
FLAMING ARROWS

AVB 71 P. L. Travers
MARY POPPINS

AVB 72 Helen F. Daringer
ADOPTED JANE

AVB 74 Elizabeth Enright
RETURN TO GONE-AWAY

AVB 76 Carolyn Haywood
BACK TO SCHOOL WITH BETSY

AVB 78 Mary Norton
THE BORROWERS AFLOAT

AVB 82 Anne Holm
NORTH TO FREEDOM

AVB 83 Mary Norton
THE BORROWERS ALOFT

AVB 85 Carl Sandburg
ROOTABAGA STORIES, Part I

AVB 90 Carl Sandburg
ROOTABAGA STORIES, Part II
Rootabaga Pigeons